Tricks and Treats

OTHER BOOKS YOU WILL ENJOY:

A CERTAIN SMALL SHEPHERD, *Rebecca Caudill*
A GIFT FOR TÍA ROSA, *Karen T. Taha*
A GRAIN OF RICE, *Helena Clare Pittman*
MOLLY'S PILGRIM, *Barbara Cohen*
MAKE A WISH, MOLLY, *Barbara Cohen*
TURKEY TROUBLE, *Patricia Reilly Giff*
THE POSTCARD PEST, *Patricia Reilly Giff*

Tricks and Treats

JUDY DELTON

Illustrated by Alan Tiegreen

A YEARLING BOOK

Published by
Bantam Doubleday Dell Books for Young Readers
a division of
Bantam Doubleday Dell Publishing Group, Inc.
1540 Broadway
New York, New York 10036

ISBN: 0-440-40976-4

Printed in the United States of America

September 1994

10 9 8 7 6

CWO

For Maureen Parsons and all of her great readers
at G. H. Nichols School in Endicott, New York,
with thanks for being friends
of the Pee Wees.

Contents

1 Mrs. Peters Forgets   1
2 No Party Plans   12
3 Double Secret   24
4 The Scariest Story of All   35
5 Molly Looks for Work   46
6 A Trick on the Pee Wees   57
7 A Happy Ending   68

CHAPTER 1

Mrs. Peters Forgets

"**A**nd remember," said Mrs. Pine, "it's safety first on Halloween night. Halloween will be here before you know it."

Mrs. Pine was Molly Duff's second grade teacher.

"We'll be having a little party here in our room before the big day!" she added.

Just then the bell rang. School was out for the day.

"Some party," said Roger White, dumping his math book in his desk. "School parties are dumb. A bunch of candy corn and apples with faces on them."

"Our Pee Wee Scout party will be better,"

1

said Rachel Meyers, putting her library book into her backpack. "Mrs. Peters knows what a real Halloween party is."

Mrs. Peters was the leader of Troop 23. They met every Tuesday afternoon in her basement.

But at the meeting the next day, Mrs. Peters did not mention Halloween. She asked for good deeds instead.

Hands waved. Maybe after good deeds, thought Molly. Then she will talk about Halloween.

"I made a birthday cake for my little sister," said Tracy Barnes.

"Good," said Mrs. Peters. "What a fine good deed! Anyone else?" She looked from one to the other.

"I raked leaves off my porch," said Tim Noon.

"Hey, you don't rake your porch, dummy!" yelled Roger. "How can you rake a floor?" Roger took a make-believe rake and raked the basement floor. He made loud scraping noises.

"There were leaves on our porch," said Tim, giving Roger a punch in the arm.

Mrs. Peters held up her hand. That meant no pushing or shoving or fighting.

"Did you sweep them?" said Mrs. Peters.

Tim shook his head. "I raked them," he said.

Rachel's hand was waving.

"Mrs. Peters, Mrs. Peters!" she called. "I baby-sat for my neighbor's Siamese cat. His name is Jeeves. He's very, very smart. I had to give him this special cat food for show cats," she added.

"He's probably some old alley cat," taunted Roger.

"You take that back, Roger White!" said Rachel. "Jeeves comes from a long line of famous show cats. He has papers."

Rachel's face was red. Roger irritated her,

thought Molly. Actually, Roger irritated everyone. That was his nature.

Mrs. Peters was still not mentioning Halloween. Maybe she needed someone to remind her. She was still looking for good deeds.

Molly raised her hand. "I helped my mom clean our attic," she said. "We packed all kinds of stuff away, like old Halloween costumes that are too small for me."

There. Now Mrs. Peters would remember the holiday that was coming up. The most important holiday of the year.

But all Mrs. Peters said was "Very good, Molly. It is always a big job to clean an attic. Your mom must have appreciated the help."

Rat's knees, thought Molly. She tapped her foot. Her idea hadn't worked.

"Maybe we aren't having any Pee Wee Halloween party," whispered Mary Beth Kelly to Molly. Mary Beth was Molly's best friend.

"Mrs. Peters wouldn't forget Halloween,"

said Patty Baker. Patty and Kenny Baker were twins. They were both Scouts. Their cousin Ashley was a temporary Pee Wee Scout. She lived in California but came to Pee Wee Scouts when she was visiting her cousins. She was back in California now.

"I washed one window for my mom," said Lisa Ronning. "That was all I could reach."

"I picked up a newspaper my dad dropped," said Roger.

The good deeds were getting weaker and weaker, thought Molly. This always happened toward the end of the announcements. Some Pee Wees would make up their good deeds.

"I picked a flower for my mom," said Sonny Stone.

"Where did you get it?" asked Roger. "Out of your neighbor's garden?"

"Out of my own garden," said Sonny.

"I'll bet it was a weed," whispered Tracy

6

"Sonny doesn't know the difference between a flower and a weed!"

Molly felt sorry for Sonny. His mother babied him. Sonny still had training wheels on his bike and he was seven. His mother had just married the fire chief and they had adopted twins, but it had not helped Sonny grow up as everyone thought it would. He was still a mama's boy, even though now he had a father.

The good deeds were over. Now Mrs. Peters would plan the party, thought Molly. But she didn't. Instead, she passed out drawing paper.

"Maybe it's for making Halloween masks!" said Lisa.

"Or pumpkins," said Kevin Moe.

Molly was going to marry Kevin someday. He was her favorite Scout.

But Mrs. Peters asked them to draw a map of the neighborhood on the paper. She held up a map of their city and said the ones they made would be smaller.

"I think Mrs. Peters forgot all about Halloween," said Mary Beth.

"How could she?" asked Molly.

Halloween was hard to ignore. There were pumpkins with mean faces in all the stores along Main Street. There were witches in the school windows. There were safety posters in the shape of goblins on the lightposts. Even some houses had ghosts and witches in the windows. Mrs. Peters would have to be blind not to notice Halloween coming.

"First draw a line down the middle of your map," she was saying. "Write 'Main Street' on it."

"Bor-ing," Lisa sighed.

Mrs. Peters showed them how to make lines crossing Main Street that were the streets the Pee Wees lived on.

"Put your school on Elm Street," she said. "And my house on Oak. And be sure to put

your own house and your neighbors' houses on too."

Molly colored her house light blue. She drew Mary Beth's house, and Sonny's, and colored them green.

"Now," said Mrs. Peters, "draw a big red line around all of the houses, like this."

She showed the Pee Wees how by holding Molly's map up in front of the room. A bright red marker line circled the houses and stores that Molly had drawn.

"Now," said Mrs. Peters, "you have a map of the streets and houses you go to on Halloween, when you go trick-or-treating."

"Yeah!" shouted the Pee Wees in relief.

"She didn't forget!" said Mary Beth.

"She tricked us," said Roger.

"I knew Halloween was too important for Mrs. Peters to ignore," said Kevin.

Kevin used bigger words than the other Pee Wees. He was smart, thought Molly.

The Pee Wees all clapped and cheered as

Mrs. Peters told them the safety rules for trick-or-treating.

"We go only to houses we know, in our own neighborhood," she said.

Sonny's mother, who was assistant troop leader, came down the steps with cupcakes.

The cupcakes were not orange and black. They were pink. And pink is not a Halloween color.

CHAPTER 2

No Party Plans

The Pee Wees ate them anyway.

After their treat the Pee Wees said their pledge. Then they sang their Pee Wee Scout song. After that, they helped clean up Mrs. Peters's yard. They played with the Peterses' baby, Nick. And with Lucky, the Pee Wee mascot.

"Now," said Mrs. Peters when all the Pee Wees had collapsed into the lawn chairs. "We all know Halloween is coming up soon."

"At last," sighed the troop. At last their leader was going to tell them about the party.

"Instead of a party this year," she went on, "I thought we would do something for others.

After all, that is what being a Scout is all about. Helping others."

The Scouts moaned. And groaned. They liked to help others. But not on Halloween. Not instead of a party.

"Rat's knees!" shouted Molly. "It's my favorite holiday!"

"Mine too!" shouted Lisa and Tracy.

"We will still dress up in costumes. And go trick-or-treating. But then I thought it would be fun to *give some treats instead of getting them.*"

The Pee Wees didn't say anything. They waited to see what Mrs. Peters had in mind.

"Many people give food to the food bank program," she went on. "And the people who need food, or are out of work, can get food there."

"My aunt goes to the food bank," said Patty.

Molly knew being poor was not a shameful

thing. Still, she would be very upset if she had to get free food.

Mrs. Peters held her hand up. "The reason I mentioned it," she said, "is because I thought it would be a good thing for the Pee Wees to hand out treats to all the children when they come with their parents to get food! We could put up signs telling people there will be free treats on that night. We could dress up and wear our costumes to give treats out, instead of taking them in! What do you think of that idea?"

The Pee Wees were cautious. Was this some kind of grown-up trick?

"Can we go trick-or-treating first?" asked Roger.

"If you want to," said Mrs. Peters.

"Then I guess it's a good idea," he said.

"Where will we get the treats to give out?" asked Lisa.

"I thought we could all donate some," said Mrs. Peters. "I know I can bring some popcorn, and Mrs. Stone will bring some candy, and I'm sure other people will donate fruit and maybe even games and toys for a special Halloween treat for the children at the food bank."

Everyone thought it was a good idea. They cheered. It would be as much fun as a party, thought Molly. Maybe more.

"And I have another surprise," Mrs. Peters went on. "There will be a prize for the best costume. But it must not be a store-bought one. It must be homemade.

"And there will be another prize for the scariest story you can make up. We will read them around a Pee Wee campfire late at night, and choose the most scary one.

"Last of all, there will be a Halloween badge for all those who give out treats at the food bank, wear a homemade costume, and tell a scary story."

"Yeah!" everyone shouted.

"This is better than a party!" said Kenny.

16

Soon the meeting was over, but the Pee Wees talked about costumes and scary stories all the way home. They talked about getting a brand-new badge and telling ghost stories around a fire.

"I wish Ashley were here for the party," said Patty.

"I'll bet Rachel is glad she isn't," whispered Mary Beth to Molly. "Rachel thinks she's a show-off."

Molly giggled. "Rachel is a show-off too," she whispered. "Ashley is too much competition for her."

"My mom isn't going to like it that we can't buy a costume," said Rachel. "Homemade stuff takes so long to make."

"Yeah," agreed Patty.

Patty and Rachel turned off at the corner. Molly and Mary Beth walked on.

"Let's work on our costumes together," said Molly.

"Tomorrow after school," agreed Mary Beth.

They couldn't start too soon for Molly. Molly liked to get things done fast. She liked to be the first one to do things or get places, and the first one to earn a new badge.

The girls said good-bye, and Molly went on to her own house to tell her parents about the Pee Wee Halloween plans.

"Well, that's a good idea," said Mr. Duff, who had just come home from work. "A party would only be more candy corn and soda pop. Bad for your teeth."

Molly laughed. "That's what Roger said. The candy corn part."

"And giving treats instead of taking them is a good thing. The people who use the food bank will appreciate that."

Molly felt warm all over thinking about how good it would feel to help hungry children. To share candy and toys with children who had none. And it wasn't even Christmas.

Christmas would be a long time to wait for a game or candy bar or apple. The Pee Wees would help now!

The next day after school, Mary Beth and Molly sat on the Kellys' front porch and planned their costumes.

"My mom says we should do a lot of thinking before we start to make them," said Mary Beth.

"We have to get stuff like material and needles and thread and scissors, and we have to measure," said Molly.

"My mom says, 'Measure twice, cut once,'" said Mary Beth.

"We wouldn't have to sew it," said Molly, thinking. "I mean, we could use Scotch tape or glue or rubber bands or safety pins to hold it together."

"The first thing we have to do is decide what we want to be," said Mary Beth. "I mean, like a ballerina or a frog or a cowboy or what."

"There are always lots of ballerinas," said Molly.

"And we couldn't *make* a ballet costume," said Mary Beth.

Rachel walked by, eating a lime Popsicle.

"I might wear my riding costume, and go as a horsewoman," she said.

"That isn't homemade," said Molly. "That is store bought."

"But it's what real horsewomen wear," said Rachel.

Molly frowned. Rachel had a good point.

"I have to go to my dance lesson," said Rachel, sighing. She waved good-bye and walked down the street.

"I want to be something different this year," said Molly. "Something no one else is."

"So do I," said Mary Beth. "Not a dumb old pumpkin or witch or ghost."

Molly's mother said she was very creative. That she had a wild imagination.

"I think I have an idea," Molly said. "For

both of us. But we can't tell anyone. Otherwise they'll copy us."

"I won't tell anyone!" said Mary Beth. "Tell me, tell me!"

Molly leaned over and whispered something in Mary Beth's ear.

"Wow!" said Mary Beth. "No one would ever think of that. Not in a million years! We'll both win. It will be a tie!"

"Let's get started right away," she said. "It's easy to make the costumes. And no one ever was one of these before. I know just where to find the right stuff to make them. Follow me."

Mary Beth led Molly up into her attic, where her mother had boxes and boxes of old scraps of material. And old clothes. And buttons and zippers and hats and feathers and all the things anyone would want to use for a costume. She found an old red blanket. "Here!" she said. "Now we need something thin and tan colored."

By the time Mary Beth's mother called her for supper, the girls had found all the things they needed. Now they just had to turn them into something else. Something that was a deep dark secret until Halloween.

CHAPTER 3

Double Secret

All week the girls cut and sewed. They sewed after school. And on Saturday and Sunday. When they had trouble sewing, they pinned. Finally the costumes were finished. The girls put them on and stood in front of the mirror.

"This is the best costume of all, and we made it ourselves!" said Mary Beth.

"Well, no one will have one like it," agreed Molly. "I think we'll win the prize."

"Let's not show it to anyone till Halloween night," said Mary Beth.

At school, Roger said he was coming as a pirate.

"Pooh," said Lisa. "That's ordinary. Pirate costumes are a dime a dozen."

"Mine's a secret," Rachel said.

"So are ours," said Molly. "We are going to win the prize."

"How can you both win the prize?" asked Rachel.

"You'll see," said Mary Beth, giggling.

At three o'clock, Molly got out her list. She kept a list of everything she wanted to do. She carefully crossed off "costume." The next thing on the list said "Write a scary story."

She decided to do this at the library. The library was quiet. There were big tables. And there were books about ghosts.

When she got there, Kevin was there too. He was writing something in a notebook. At another table was Lisa. She was writing too.

Molly got some books about scary things. She looked through them. Then she sat down to write. But she couldn't think of how to start. Finally she wrote "It was a scary night.

It was raining and thundering and lightning." She couldn't think of what to write next.

Lisa was writing and writing. But it looked as if she was copying something out of the library book. Molly did not want to copy. Mrs. Peters said they were to make up a story, not copy one. Kevin was writing fast too. But he was not copying. He waved to Molly. Molly went to his table.

"This is such a scary story, I'm even scared writing it," he whispered.

"I can't think of anything scary," whispered Molly back. But Kevin was writing so fast, he didn't even hear her.

Molly took her paper and folded it up and started for home. On the way she stopped at her best friend's house.

"I can't think of a scary story," she told Mary Beth.

"Mine is all finished," said her friend. "My aunt helped me."

Molly did not want to cheat. But she didn'

want to be the only one without a scary story
She wasn't worried about her costume. O
about giving out treats at the food bank. Bu
to get her badge, she had to have a story t
read or tell around the campfire.

When Molly left Mary Beth's, Tim was jus
coming from school. Why was she worrying
about being the only one with no story? Tin
could not write a story either, she bet. Sh
asked him.

"I've got my story ready," he said.

Molly's spirits fell. Even Tim was ahead o
her with this.

"Do you want to hear it?"

Before Molly could say yes or no, Tim said
" 'Once we had a burglar in the middle of th
night, but really it was my uncle.' "

Molly waited. And waited. "Well?" sh
said. "Tell me the scary story."

"I just did," said Tim. "That's it."

So Tim's story was one line long. And i
was not scary. But Molly did not want a one

ine story. Or a copied story. Or an aunt's tory. She wanted a badge, but she did not vant it enough to cut corners.

"Rat's knees!" she said.

When she got home, she crumpled up the ainy night story and threw it into the waste-asket. She began again. Then she threw that ne away. She wondered how people wrote vhole books. With lots of pages. She decided he would never be a writer. Even though at chool her teacher brought in authors who nade writing sound easy and fun.

Molly's mother called her for dinner. After linner, she reminded Molly to do her home-vork. After that it was bedtime.

I'll think about it tomorrow, she said to her-elf.

But tomorrow was Pee Wee meeting day.

The first thing their leader said was, "I hope ou are all working hard on your costumes nd scary stories! Next Saturday is the big ay!"

29

"Mine's done, Mrs. Peters," called Tim.

"Mine too," cried Rachel and Roger and Kevin and Lisa.

A few of the other Pee Wees were not ready yet, but that did not make Molly feel any better. She liked to be fast. And she liked to be best. It did not bother Tracy and Sonny that time was passing and they might not get badges. They never thought of things until the last minute, and sometimes not even then. And in the end they usually got their badges anyway!

It's not fair, thought Molly to herself.

"Today," smiled Mrs. Peters, "we are going to plan what treats we'll give out at the food bank. I'd like to get an idea of what you each can bring so we won't run out of treats. I've talked to some of your mothers and fathers about this, and if you can tell me what your treat is and how many you can bring, I'll write it down. Remember, this is for the children who may not have any treats at home. So i you can save your allowance and buy or bake something yourself, that would be even better."

Hands waved.

"My dad called you, Mrs. Peters," said Tracy. "He is making three pans of fudge, with nuts."

"Wonderful," said their leader.

"I'm going to buy real candy bars with my own money," said Roger. "Ten of them."

"Good for you," said Mrs. Peters, writing it down.

"I'm bringing popcorn balls. Red ones," said Patty.

"Yuck," said Roger.

Rachel's hand was waving. "Mrs. Peters," she said, "my parents are donating a carton of sugarless chewing gum."

"Wow, a carton," said Kenny. "That's a lot of gum."

"But it's sugarless," said Roger. "Dentists don't believe in real candy."

"That is very generous, Rachel," said Mrs. Peters.

Molly's mother had said she would make brownies, plenty for everyone. At least Molly would not fail at this project. She would not come empty-handed.

After everything was written down, Mrs. Peters said, "It looks like we will have plenty of treats!"

Patty raised her hand. "Won't it be embarrassing for the kids to take our stuff?" she asked.

Mrs. Peters frowned. "We have to make them comfortable," she said. "Perhaps one of their parents is out of work, or they have doctors' bills. The food bank is for anyone who needs it. There is no reason for anyone to be embarrassed. Besides, the things we give out are like trick-or-treat candies."

"I'm glad I don't have to worry about using the food bank," said Lisa.

"So am I," said Roger.

Molly didn't say anything out loud. But she was glad she had a home and food too. And a mother who made brownies.

The Pee Wees ate their cupcakes and sang their song and said their pledge. Then it was time to go home. Molly didn't want to think about being poor. She ran all the way home, with an idea for her scary story. But when she went in the back door, she forgot all about it. Her mother and father were talking about something. Something that sounded like bad news. Her mother had tears in her eyes. They both looked sad.

Mrs. Duff put her arm around Molly's shoulder and said, "Daddy lost his job today, Molly."

When her mother said her name at the end of a sentence, it was serious. Forget about writing a scary story. Molly was *in* a scary story, right this minute!

CHAPTER 4

The Scariest Story
of All

Molly's ears were ringing with her mother's words. *"Daddy lost his job."* Her dad, who always smiled, was not smiling now. He did not kid Molly and tickle her under the chin and try to make her laugh.

He looked up from his chair and said, "Don't worry, honey. It's not the end of the world. I'll get another job."

But he didn't look as if he believed it.

Molly ran to her room and threw herself on her bed. Her family was poor! It was the thing she dreaded the most. The thing they had just talked about. And it had happened.

How could she tell the Pee Wees? Would

she be *getting* treats from her friends on Halloween, instead of handing them out? Would it be a backward Halloween?

She pictured herself in line taking treats gratefully from Mary Beth and Roger and Sonny and the others. Some of the Pee Wees were feeling sorry for her. Some of them were *laughing* at her!

Her mother and father would be there getting free food from the food bank.

Molly felt tears spilling out of her eyes and running down her face. She did not smell any dinner cooking downstairs. Maybe they were poor already! Maybe her mother had no money for food, and they would starve! Molly remembered seeing pictures of starving children in other countries.

Suddenly Molly felt sorry for her father. If she felt this bad, he must feel worse. She had to help somehow. Could she find her dad a new job? Could she get a job herself to help out? There were no jobs for seven-year-olds.

She knew for a fact you had to be sixteen to work for money.

"Molly," called her mother from downstairs, "come and eat dinner!"

So they had food after all! Molly ran downstairs and gave her dad a hug. Then she sat down at the table as on any other evening. Her dad opened a bag of take-out hamburgers and french fries. Usually they had take-out to celebrate something. But this was nothing to celebrate.

"I couldn't think of anything to make," said Mrs. Duff. "So Dad got hamburgers."

The burgers seemed dry to Molly and stuck in her throat. She wasn't hungry and wished she didn't have to eat.

"Are we going to starve?" The words burst out of Molly.

"Of course not, honey," said her dad, patting Molly on the head. "We might have to use the food bank if we're in a pinch. And we'll have to cut back on our spending. But it's nothing for you to worry about."

How could her dad say that? Of course it was something for her to worry about! It was her own family!

When her dad kissed her good night, he looked sad. And when her mother tucked her in bed, she forgot to turn Molly's night-light on. Things had definitely changed in the Duff family.

At school the next morning everyone acted the same. Molly's friends acted as if Molly were the person she was yesterday. They did not know that she was poor and would not be handing out treats with the rest of them.

At recess Mary Beth said, "Do you want me to help you write your scary story?"

Molly had forgotten all about the story. She wanted to cry and tell Mary Beth that the story wasn't important now. She wanted help with fixing her family, not with her story. But she didn't say that. She said, "I can do it, but thanks anyway."

On the way home from school, the Pee Wees were talking about their costumes.

"I can't wait till Halloween," said Sonny.

"My dad's got the fudge all made," said Mary Beth.

"I'm going to get the prize for the scariest story," said Tracy.

"We're going trick-or-treating first, aren't we, Molly?" said Mary Beth.

All of a sudden Molly burst into tears. The other Pee Wees stopped talking and stared. They were surprised. Molly never cried!

"What's the matter with you?" asked Sonny. "Have you got a cramp? My cousin got a cramp once, and it was appendicitis."

Mary Beth put her arm around her friend. So did Rachel.

"Are your feelings hurt?" asked Mary Beth.

"My dad lost his job," shouted Molly in relief. "We're poor, and we have to get food at

40

the food bank. And I won't be able to hand out treats with you on Halloween."

None of the Pee Wees knew what to say, so they didn't say anything.

"He can get a new job," said Mary Beth finally. "My aunt did when she lost her job. An even better one."

Molly just shook her head and kept crying. She couldn't stop.

"That's awful," said Sonny. "I feel sorry for you."

Molly knew Sonny meant to be kind. But she didn't want pity. Especially from Sonny. She didn't want to be different. She broke away from the others and ran all the way home and in her back door.

"Why, Molly, what's the matter with you?" asked her mother. "You look all hot and dirty!"

Her mother pulled her over onto her lap.

"We're poor," Molly blurted out. "I can't

41

give out treats on Halloween because we won't have money."

Her mother listened to her, then said, "Things are bad, but not that bad. I'm sorry we worried you so much, but Dad just found out yesterday and we were shocked. I'm still working, you know, and we have some money saved, and Dad will find something else soon. Meanwhile, we have lots of food in the freezer, and it will be fun to have Dad around the house more. We'll just pinch some pennies and get along the best we can. We are all together, and we have a nice warm house, and there's nothing for you to worry about."

"Really?" said Molly, wiping her eyes.

Her mother nodded. "You can give out treats with the others just as you planned. Life doesn't change overnight. Lots of people who bring food to the food bank have to use it sometimes."

"Aren't we poor?" asked Molly.

Her mother laughed. "Not yet," she said.

"Sometimes being poor is in your mind and not your body, you know."

Just then the doorbell rang. Molly washed her face while her mother answered it.

"It's for you, Molly," she called.

Molly went to the door. It was Rachel. She handed Molly an apple pie. "My mom made it," she said.

Rachel stood and shuffled her feet. Rachel wasn't usually nervous. "My mom says after my dad finished dental school, he couldn't get a job, and our friends shared a lot of stuff with us. It took a long time before he got a good job."

"Really?" said Molly. "You were POOR?" She couldn't picture Rachel poor. Rachel without dance lessons and lots of clothes.

Rachel nodded. "Of course, I was real little. I don't really remember it."

Molly felt warm toward Rachel. She asked her to come in.

Rachel called her mother and asked if she

43

could stay for supper. By the time she left, Molly felt much better. She didn't feel as if she had a sign around her neck that said "I am poor." And her friends liked her anyway!

Before she went to bed, she called Mary Beth. "I wrote my scary story," she said. "It's about a girl who finds out her family is real poor and then her brother wins the lottery."

"What's scary about that?" asked Mary Beth. "There are no ghosts or spirits in it."

Molly sighed. "You've never been poor," she told her patiently. "It's the scariest thing in the world! But I gave it a happy ending."

"Well, it sounds good," said Mary Beth. "But I don't think it's scary enough to win the prize."

Whether she won or not, Molly felt better. And she was glad her story was finished.

CHAPTER **5**

Molly Looks for Work

The Pee Wees counted the days left till Halloween. Then they counted the hours. And the minutes. Molly had her costume ready. She had her scary story ready. She would be able to hand out treats at the food bank with the others. There was only one more thing she wanted that she didn't have. That was a job for her father. Her mother said it was nothing for Molly to worry about. Her dad said he would take care of it himself. But could he?

A few days before Halloween, Molly and Mary Beth put up a card table on Mary Beth's front porch. They got out scissors and paste and decorated trick-or-treat bags to carry their candy in. They cut pumpkins out of orange paper and pasted them on brown grocery bags. They cut out witches on broomsticks and flying ghosts and pasted those on too.

"I think I should look for a job for my dad," said Molly to her friend.

"You can't apply for a job for a grown-up!" said Mary Beth.

"I know," said Molly. "But I could look around and find a job and tell him about it."

"Where can you look?" asked Mary Beth. "What kind of work can he do?"

"He can do anything," said Molly. "My dad is real smart."

"That should be easy, then," said Mary Beth. "We will just look for signs that say 'Help wanted.' "

"We can even look in the paper!" said Molly.

Mary Beth ran to get the newspaper. She turned to the want ads.

Help Wanted said the words at the top of a column. Molly ran her finger down the list.

" 'Night nurses wanted,' " read Mary Beth. "Can your dad be a nurse?"

"Of course," said Molly.

"Let's call this number," said Mary Beth. She dialed, and Molly talked. She told the person at the other end that Mr. Duff was interested in the job.

"Is he qualified?" asked the voice. Molly did not know what qualified was, but she knew her dad could do it.

"Yes," she said.

"Have him pick up an application," said the voice.

"I'll pick it up," said Molly. She wrote down the address. It was not far from her house.

"There!" said Molly, hanging up the phone. "It's all taken care of."

Mary Beth frowned. "You can't be sure," she said. "Lots of people are looking for jobs.

And maybe we better find some more, so that he has a choice. Maybe he won't want to be a nurse."

What a good idea Mary Beth had! Molly would never have thought of that! She did not think her father should be so fussy—after all, a job was a job—but Mary Beth might be right.

"Look, the Burger Buddy needs a cook!" said Mary Beth. "Can your dad cook?"

Molly frowned. She had to think. She remembered when her father put an apron on and cut the Thanksgiving turkey. And sometimes he made breakfast for the Duffs. And when they had hamburgers on the grill, her father always cooked them.

"Yes!" said Molly.

Mary Beth dialed the number. "We have someone who will take your job as a cook," she said in a very businesslike tone. Then she said yes and no and maybe to some questions.

50

"We can pick up the blank," said Mary Beth. "You dad will have lots of jobs."

The girls called a few more phone numbers. One was for a veterinarian.

"My dad loves dogs!" said Molly.

Another was for a law firm. "Your dad always obeys all the laws, doesn't he?" asked Mary Beth.

Molly nodded. Mr. Duff always stopped at red lights. And he never crossed the street in the middle of the block—he always went to the corner.

"I think he should take the law job," said Mary Beth.

"But he likes dogs," said Molly. "And he's a good cook."

"We'll let him decide," said Mary Beth.

"Won't he be surprised when he finds out he has a job?" said Molly.

"I don't think we should tell him," said Mary Beth. "I think it should be a surprise."

It would be a good Halloween surprise.

Mary Beth was right again! Molly wondered why she had ever been so worried about being poor. There were all kinds of jobs for her father!

When the girls finished their trick-or-treat bags, they collected the application blanks. They walked the long way through downtown so they could look at the Halloween decorations in the store windows.

"Look," said Mary Beth, stopping at the corner. She pointed to a bulletin board in the bank window. HELP WANTED it said.

The girls walked over and read the notices. Some were for baby-sitters and dog-walkers. Some were for carry-out clerks at the grocery store. And some were for help in the bank itself.

"Applications Inside" it said. The girls went in. When they came out, Molly had five more forms for her father to fill out.

"The banks have the most money," said

Mary Beth. "You would be rich if your dad takes that job."

When Molly got home, she put the forms on her dad's desk. She put them under a pile of papers so they would be a surprise.

Finally it was Halloween. As soon as school was out, the Pee Wees got ready to go trick-or-treating.

"We have to wait till it's dark," said Sonny. "Otherwise it isn't scary."

"You'd be scared of your own shadow, Stone," said Roger. "I'll bet your mama is going trick-or-treating with you."

"So what," muttered Sonny. "She has to take the twins anyway. I have to go along and help her."

"Ha!" laughed Roger. "You're going along because you're scared of the goblins."

"Am not," said Sonny.

"Are too," said Roger.

"We'll meet you guys at the park," said Lisa.

"See you there," said Rachel.

Right after supper, the Pee Wees met at the park. They had their costumes on and their bags in hand. Kevin had a flashlight. And he had glow-in-the-dark patches on his costume.

"It's for safety," he said. "So the cars can see me crossing the streets."

The Pee Wees had the maps they had drawn. They would go only to houses they knew. Sonny's mother was there with the twins in a stroller. They were dressed up as twin angels. They even had silver foil halos. Mrs. Stone was an angel too. Her halo bounced up and down as she walked. Sonny was a red devil. He had a long red tail and two red horns on the top of his head. He carried a black pitchfork in his hand. It was made out of cardboard. He ran after Roger with it.

"Get out of here, Stone!" Roger cried, chasing Sonny with his pirate's sword.

Roger had a black patch over one eye and a

rag tied around his head that had red paint on it. The paint was supposed to be blood.

Molly and Mary Beth came running up late.

"Where are your costumes?" asked Rachel. Everyone stared at the two girls. They were the only ones not in costume.

"We can't wear it till after trick-or-treating," said Mary Beth.

"Why not?" asked Patty.

The girls giggled. "Just wait and see," they said.

CHAPTER 6

A Trick on the Pee Wees

"**H**ey, Meyers, you didn't *make* that costume!" shouted Roger, pointing to Rachel's riding outfit. She had on jodhpurs and riding boots and a black riding hat. "No way is that homemade," said Roger again. "You can't win if you bought your costume. Can you, Mrs. Stone?"

Mrs. Stone didn't hear him because the twins were crying loudly. They were afraid of the pirate.

"It's what real riders wear," snapped Rachel. "So I still can win."

The Pee Wees all started to argue about if handmade was homemade. Molly did **not** care if Rachel won. Rachel had been poor. She knew how Molly felt, having a father without a job. Rachel deserved to win, no matter where her costume came from.

All the costumes were good. Molly had been sure she would win. But now she saw that lots of the costumes were as good as hers.

Patty and Kenny Baker were dressed like the TV cartoon characters Tom and Jerry. Patty was the little gray furry mouse, and Kenny was the cat. He even had whiskers.

Tom began to chase Jerry around a tree. Then the pirate chased the red devil down the street. The trick-or-treat bags flapped in the wind.

Mrs. Stone left to take the twins home. "I'll see you all at the food bank in one hour," she said. "It will still be light then. Be sure to go to only the houses you know."

When Mrs. Stone left, Roger said, "I wish it was dark. It's not scary in the daylight."

"We couldn't go out alone after dark," said

Tim. "We'd have to have some grown-ups along, and that's no fun."

The Pee Wees all agreed grown-ups were no fun.

"I don't think we should all go to the same houses," said Roger. "I mean all together. They won't give us as many treats."

"I think we should go all together," said Tracy, who was dressed like a rock star. "That's what the Pee Wees are all about. Doing things together."

"Yeah," said Kevin. "That's right."

So all the Pee Wees walked down the street together. They all trooped onto the porches together. And they all shouted "Trick or treat!" together when the door opened.

At the first house, they got a peppermint stick each.

"I'll bet these are left over from last Christmas," said Tracy.

At the next house, they all got orange popcorn balls.

And at Mrs. Mill's drugstore, they all got candy bars.

"Let's go to that big house up on the hill," said Tim, pointing. "Those people are real rich. I'll bet they give out money."

The Pee Wees looked at the house. "We don't know them," said Molly. "We can't go to people we don't know. They may be criminals."

"My uncle's boss lives there," said Lisa, who had on a bridal dress with a real veil. "He came to our house for dinner once. James Somebody."

"That's good enough," said Roger. The Pee Wees all agreed.

"The house looks haunted," said Mary Beth.

"Naw," said Roger. "It's just big and old."

The Pee Wees walked up the hill. They got closer and closer. The wind whistled in the trees. There was a wailing sound.

"What's that?" asked Tracy. "It sounds like a ghost."

"It isn't even dark," said Rachel. "No ghost comes out in the sunlight."

But the sun was going behind a cloud, Molly noticed. It looked as if it might rain.

When the Pee Wees got to the door, Roger rang the bell. Everyone looked nervous. Suddenly the door flew open, and a lady with lots of jewelry on stood there. Molly counted her rings. On one hand alone she had five! With real diamonds, Molly was sure.

"That's not my uncle's boss!" said Lisa.

The Pee Wees were so surprised, they forgot what they were there for. Then they remembered. It was too late to leave now. The woman had answered the door. The woman who was not Lisa's uncle's boss!

"Trick or treat!" they shouted. "Money or eats!"

"What sweet little children!" said the lady.

"My name is Mrs. Hudson. Won't you come in?"

The Pee Wees looked at each other. No one else had invited trick-or-treaters in. Was it safe? Why did she want them to come in?

It seemed impolite to refuse, thought Molly. But she remembered what Mrs. Stone had said: "Go only to the homes of people you know."

"Is this where James Somebody lives?" asked Lisa.

"James is my son," said Mrs. Hudson. Lisa told Mrs. Hudson about her uncle. It's safe, thought Molly. She stepped inside the door. Not all of the other Pee Wees followed. Molly noticed that Tim and Lisa and Tracy hung back. Then they turned and ran down the steps and down the hill. Molly half wished she had run too.

"Now," said Mrs. Hudson. "Sit down and tell me your names!"

Each Pee Wee said her or his name for Mrs.

Hudson. Her bracelets were jingling and jangling. Molly had never seen such a big living room. It was as big as her whole house.

"Now," said Mrs. Hudson, "You must each do something for your treat. Do you have some talent you can show us?"

Molly started to panic. She had no talent! What would she do?

"I don't like this," whispered Mary Beth. "I want to go."

"I'll bet she locked the door!" said Patty.

"We don't have to work for our treats at other houses," said Sonny. He looked like he wanted to cry. "She tricked us!"

Rachel began to tap-dance, even though she had her riding outfit on and no music.

The lady clapped. "Why, that is wonderful!" she said. "Who wants to be next?"

The Pee Wees were all feeling angry at Lisa, who had an uncle who knew this lady's son. It was her fault they were trapped here on the best day of the year.

"I don't have any talent," said Molly.

"Come, come, don't be modest. Everyone has a talent," laughed the lady.

What would she do if they didn't perform? wondered Molly. Would she lock them up? Put them in a bubbly stew?

Now real tears were rolling down Sonny's face. They made his costume wet. The wet made the material fade. Soon his whole face was streaked red from the devil suit dye.

Patty was singing a song, but she looked scared to death. When she finished, Kevin counted up to ten in Spanish and recited the Presidents of the United States in order.

Molly was so impressed, she knew she had to marry Kevin. He was the smartest one in the Pee Wees. In her school. In the world!

"I can count up to ten!" said Sonny, waving his hand.

"In what language?" asked Roger.

"English," said Sonny.

Roger hooted and hollered at this. "Who

can't, dummy? I'll bet your baby sisters can too!"

But Sonny did it, and so did all the other Pee Wees, and Mrs. Hudson laughed a light musical laugh like her tinkling bracelets. She said, "I think you have all worked very hard for your treat."

"This better be good," muttered Roger.

Mrs. Hudson stood up and handed each Pee Wee a dollar bill!

They all thanked her and filed out the door, and Mrs. Hudson called, "Come again! Come to see me whenever you like!"

"Not on your life," said Sonny. "I'm not going back to that place again!"

"It wasn't so bad, and Tim was right—they did give out money!" said Roger.

All the Pee Wees agreed it wasn't scary now that they were safely out, and that the money was a better treat than a candy cane.

When they met Tim and Tracy, Roger said, "We got money!"

"And we met this real nice lady," said Kenny.

"You should have seen her fancy house," said Rachel.

The two were sorry they had run away. "Darn," said Tim. "I knew they gave out money!"

The Pee Wees went to a few more houses and then decided the hour was up and it was time to go to the food bank. But first Mary Beth and Molly had to run home and get their costumes on.

Would they have a chance at winning the prize?

CHAPTER 7
A Happy Ending

Molly and Mary Beth hurried into their costumes. It was not an easy job. The costumes had to be tight-fitting to look right.

Molly pulled and tugged.

Mary Beth pulled and tugged too.

"It's hard to breathe in here!" said Mary Beth in a muffled voice.

"I can't see anything!" shouted Molly.

"Maybe it's on backward," said Mary Beth.

Sure enough, when Molly scrambled out of the costume and turned it around, she found the eye holes. She could see and breathe.

Soon both girls were ready. They ran to the

food bank. When they went in, the other Pee Wees stared.

"What are you?" asked Sonny.

"You can't give out treats in that," said Rachel.

"I know what they are," shouted Roger. "You two are a Popsicle! A cherry Popsicle. One of you is in each side of it!"

"Hey, give me a bite!" shouted Sonny.

"Let's break this Popsicle in half," said Roger, wrestling the Popsicle to the floor.

"Leave us alone!" shouted Molly in a muffled voice. "You're going to rip our costume."

Mrs. Peters, who was Santa Claus (baby Nick was an elf), laughed and said, "That is a very good costume, girls. It is very creative. You look good enough to eat on a hot day."

"I thought of it when I saw Rachel eating a Popsicle," said Molly. "The only thing is, we just have one hand each to use."

"That's why you didn't wear your costume

trick-or-treating!" said Patty. "I'll bet you can't hand out treats with it on, either."

But Molly and Mary Beth did. Mrs. Kelly showed them how they could make a little hole in the middle of their costume to put their hands out. She cut the costume neatly with a pocket knife. But they did have to go everywhere together.

"Like Siamese twins!" said Kevin. "You have to move together!"

Molly and Mary Beth could not move much anyway because their legs were in tan stockings, one each. These were the sticks of the Popsicle.

So Kevin had noticed her! Maybe he liked her. Molly hoped that he thought that she was creative. A mayor would have to have a smart wife someday. Or a smart husband. It was a long way off, but it wasn't too soon to plan.

Molly and Mary Beth looked out of small holes in the Popsicle. They were so small, they could not be seen unless the other Pee Wees looked very hard.

"I'm hot," said Mary Beth. All the Pee Wees looked hot. "Halloween should be in January," said Molly, "when it's cold out."

Molly's parents were there giving out canned goods. The Kellys were putting apples in bags. Other parents weighed potatoes and saw that the grown-ups got what they needed.

While adults got pumpkins for pies and other food at one counter, the Pee Wees handed out lots of treats to the children at another. After the Pee Wees gave out the treats, Mrs. Peters gave each child an animal mask. Mrs. Stone helped them put the masks on.

There were little children and big children. Thin ones and fat ones. Tiny babies in strollers and toddlers walking and running. There was lots of noise and lots of crying. Sonny's twins were there playing with all of the children. Nick was there too. Even Lucky, the Pee Wee mascot, was there looking for a treat. Everyone was having a good time together.

It was just getting dark when the last customers came. Just about all the treats were gone. What was left, Mrs. Peters divided up among the Pee Wees for all their hard work.

"That was as much fun as a party," said Mary Beth.

"I guess so," muttered Roger. "Anyway, now we get to go over to the Peterses' and scare old Sonny with horror stories!"

Roger came after Sonny like a monster, snorting and growling.

"You don't scare me," boasted Sonny.

"Just wait," said Roger.

The Pee Wees helped their parents clean up the room. They picked up wrappers and candy, and Mr. Duff swept the floor. When the room was all in order, they turned out the lights and locked the doors. It was time for the Halloween bonfire and scary stories.

In the Peterses' big backyard, Mr. Peters

had the fire all laid. Larry Stone, the fire chief, lit it and showed the Pee Wees how far back to sit. "Remember, never light a fire by yourselves. Ask an adult to make sure it's a safe thing to do," he said. The Pee Wees nodded.

"Hey, we don't have to worry about this fire," shouted Tim. "Sonny's dad is fire chief!"

Mrs. Peters gathered the Pee Wees in a big circle around the fire. There was no light except for the firelight. It shone on the Pee Wees' faces. With all the masks and costumes, it was very scary, thought Molly. Even without the stories. The firelight made the colors in the costumes flash. The cherry Popsicle looked even redder than it was. Somewhere an owl hooted. And there was another sound like a wolf call.

"It's probably just a dog," said Mary Beth to Molly. But she didn't sound as if she was sure.

Mrs. Peters began the scary stories by reading a poem called "The Goblins Will Get You

If You Don't Watch Out!" by an author called James Whitcomb Riley. Afterward, Roger said, "Boo!" right behind Sonny. Sonny jumped, and the Pee Wees laughed.

"Don't you do that again, White!" said Sonny, who was shaking.

Molly told her story first. The story about the poor girl who did not have food to eat or a house to live in. "Then her brother won the lottery and they bought a house and food and lived happily ever after."

"That's not scary!" said Sonny.

"It is too," said Tim.

"But it's got a happy ending," said Sonny.

Molly didn't care if they didn't think it was scary. It was scary to her. And she had made it up, and she had told it!

Sonny told his one-line story, and everyone laughed. So far nothing was really, really scary.

But then Kevin told his story. It was about a haunted house. The people in the house were

afraid to go to sleep at night because there were tap-tap-taps at the window. And from under the bed came a low moaning sound! There was a bloody hand on the piano and a voice outside the back door that said "Get out of my house" over and over again!

Kevin lowered his voice when the ghosts talked. He made all the moaning and voice noises so well that Molly was really scared. All of the Pee Wees looked over their shoulder for a ghost.

"I'm going to be afraid to go to bed tonight!" said Rachel.

"So am I," said Molly.

The story got scarier and scarier, and it seemed to get darker and darker outside. The moon was just a sliver, and the fire snapped and crackled. It flickered and made shadows that looked like Kevin's ghosts. Every single Pee Wee was scared, and even some of the parents!

When Kevin told how the creature broke in

the back door and drove the people out, Sonny burst into tears.

"I want to go home!" he cried. "I hate this story!"

"Ho, Stone, if you go home, those creatures could be waiting for you there!" said Roger.

"I want my mother!" shouted Sonny, with more red dye from his red devil costume running over his skin. He got up and crawled over all the Pee Wees and ran to find his mother.

"What a baby!" said Rachel.

"It isn't his fault," said Molly. "Roger should leave him alone."

"He was crying before Roger said anything!" said Kenny.

"Well, I guess it proves who had the scariest story," said Lisa. "Mine wasn't scary at all compared to Kevin's."

"Neither was mine," said Mary Beth. "And my aunt helped me."

They were right. There were a few more stories, but everyone knew who would get the prize.

When the stories were over, Mrs. Peters suggested a songfest. She led the Pee Wees in one song after another. She ended up with the Pee Wee Scout song. All the Pee Wees joined hands and sang this song the loudest and clearest of all.

Molly felt warm and loving toward all her good friends. She had told her story and made her costume, and if only her father had one of those jobs she found, she would be perfectly happy.

Halloween was just about over. The Pee Wees filed into the Peterses' house for hot chocolate, while Larry put out the fire.

While everyone was drinking their drinks and comparing their treats, Mrs. Peters announced the prizes.

"All of your costumes are very good," she said. "They are wonderful. But I have to give the prize to Molly and Mary Beth because theirs is so original."

The Pee Wees clapped and clapped. Molly and Mary Beth went up to get their prize. They each got a giant box of crayons, seventy-two apiece.

Molly loved new crayons. They had the paper still wrapped around them, and all of their points were sharp. And she loved winning.

"I think we all know whose story was the scariest," laughed Mrs. Peters, calling Kevin's name. He came to get his prize. His prize was a new red notebook.

Molly looked at Sonny. He was sitting on his mother's lap with his face buried in her shirt. Poor Sonny did not seem to be having a good time, even on Halloween, the best day of the year.

"And now!" said Mrs. Peters. "The most important thing!" She held up a neat pile of badges over her head. "Our Halloween

badges for helping others. All of you made it a happy Halloween for everyone."

Everyone got a badge. After all Molly's worry, she had a wonderful badge with a big orange pumpkin on it. Why did she always worry more than anyone else? she wondered. In the end she always got her badge. She had not missed one yet! She had to grow up and not panic so easily. She was too young to worry so much.

By the time everyone said good-bye and went home, it was very late.

"This is the latest Molly has ever been out!" said her father. "Even later than New Year's Eve."

Just before she went up to bed, she overheard her father say to her mother, "I can't understand where all these job applications are coming from. I got some more in today's mail. There were even some on my desk. Do you know anything about them?"

Molly decided she would have to tell her dad.

"I wanted to help," she said. "There were lots of ads in the paper, so I called them. They all can use you! You can take your choice of those jobs."

Mr. and Mrs. Duff smiled.

"Your dad can't do all these things," said her mother. "You have to have training if you want to be a nurse. Your dad has training in accounting."

Molly's face fell. It wouldn't be as easy as she thought to get her dad a job. She did not see any ads for accounting jobs. Did she have to start worrying all over again?

"I appreciate the help," said her dad. "But I think I have something. It's not for sure, so we didn't want to tell you yet. But it looks promising."

"Really?" shouted Molly, giving her parents both a hug.

Maybe it wasn't a job that she found,

thought Molly. But her dad had a job. Or an almost-job. If he didn't get this one, he would find another by himself. Maybe not right away. But he would. Molly knew that. Her last worry was almost over.

She crawled in between her clean white sheets and fell asleep right away. She did not think of ghosts and goblins under her bed or outside the windows. And she did not dream about them either.

Not even once.

Pee Wee Scout Song

(to the tune of
"Old MacDonald Had a Farm")

Scouts are helpers, Scouts have fun
Pee Wee, Pee Wee Scouts!
We sing and play when work is done,
Pee Wee, Pee Wee Scouts!

With a good deed here,
And an errand there,
Here a hand, there a hand,
Everywhere a good hand.

Scouts are helpers, Scouts have fun,
Pee Wee, Pee Wee Scouts!

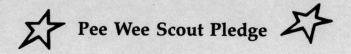

Pee Wee Scout Pledge

We love our country
And our home,
Our school and neighbors too.

As Pee Wee Scouts
We pledge our best
In everything we do.

Happy Birthday, Mallory!

For my agent, Susie Cohen—
All my love and thanks
—L. B. F.

For my husband Paul
—T. S.

Happy Birthday, Mallory!

by Laurie Friedman

illustrations by Tamara Schmitz

Carolrhoda Books, Inc. / Minneapolis

CONTENTS

 A Word from Mallory.... 6

 A Perfect Plan.... 8

 Mallory on a Mission.... 20

 Sadder Day.... 34

 The Hole Story.... 42

 Half-Birthdays.... 52

 Party Pooped.... 66

 Mallory Gets a Makeover.... 80

A Pajama Party.... 93

 Highs and Woes.... 105

 Birthday Wishes.... 114

 Mallory on Her Own.... 122

 Surprises!.... 134

 The Rest of the Hole Story.... 151

 Mallory's Party Planning Kit.... 156

A WORD FROM MALLORY

Some people might say eight is great, but for me, eight was a really, really, really hard year. Just about everything in my life changed.

First, I had to move to a new town and leave behind my best friend, Mary Ann. Then I had to go to a new school. And to top things off, my big brother, Max, got a dog even though we already had a cat . . . my cat, Cheeseburger.

But now I'm turning nine, and I know nine will be just fine because I'm planning to make nine the best year ever.

And to kick it off, I'm planning the best-ever celebration.

It all started tonight when Grandma called.

"I can't believe that in one month, my little Honey Bee will be nine years old. That's so exciting ... I bet you can hardly wait!"

And when Grandma said the part about me being hardly able to wait, I started thinking ... maybe I shouldn't wait. Maybe I should start celebrating right away.

The more I thought about it, the more I liked the idea. So I made a decision: Starting tomorrow, I'm going to start celebrating.

For my ninth birthday, I'm not going to just celebrate my birth day. I'm going to celebrate my birth *month!*

And that's when I realized, I'd better get busy. A birth month celebration takes a lot of planning. But I have a feeling if I plan it all out, it will be the world's best, best, best birth month ever.

Because if you plan it all out, nothing can go wrong.

Right?

A PERFECT PLAN

"Mom, Dad, wake up!" I bounce on my parents' bed until they start to move. "Do you know what day it is today?"

Mom opens her eyes, but she looks confused. "Monday?"

"It's Monday," I say. "But do you know why this Monday is different than all other Mondays?"

Dad rolls over and looks at the clock on his nightstand. "Mallory, on all other Mondays, we wake up at seven o'clock. It's 6:15 in the morning! What is so important about this Monday that you needed to wake us up so early?"

I plop down on the bed between Mom and Dad. "Today is the first day of my birth month celebration!"

I wait for my parents to say, *"Wow, the first day of your birth month celebration. That is so,*

so, so exciting!" But that's not what they say.

"What's a birth month celebration?" mumbles Dad.

"It's when you celebrate the *month* you were born, not just the *day*," I tell him.

Dad rolls his pillow into a ball and puts his head back on it. "Mallory, a *day* celebration is plenty."

"But I want my ninth year to be the best ever, so I'm planning to start it off with the best-ever celebration." I pull a sheet of paper out of one of my slippers and unfold it. "And I think I've come up with a perfect plan."

Mom sits up in bed and turns on a light. Dad sits up too. They look at each other, and then they look at me. "What did you have in mind?" Dad asks me.

I snuggle up between my parents and tell them exactly what I have in mind.

10 Ways I, Mallory McDonald, Plan to Celebrate My 9th Birth Month.

Way #1: By eating ALL the junk food I want.

Way #2: By watching TV for as long as I'd like.

Way #3: By staying home from school on Fridays.

Way #4: By painting my room light purple. (Dad can help.)

Way #5: By not doing my chores. (Max can help.)

Way #6: By getting my ears pierced. (V.I.W.) Very Important Way!

Way #7: By celebrating with a gift-of-the-day.

Way #8: By having a surprise party.

Way #9: By Mary Ann coming to visit on my birthday.

Way #10: By celebrating with a cake-of-the-week.

When I finish reading my list, my parents look at each other like they just came out of a parent-teacher conference, and there's something they need to talk to me about.

"Mallory," says Mom. "I know you're excited about turning nine. But we need to go through your list and talk about what's reasonable and what's unreasonable."

"I already went through my list," I tell Mom. "I crossed off the unreasonable stuff, like putting a hot fudge fountain in the backyard."

Mom reaches for my list. "I think we better do this together."

Mom looks at my list. "Mallory, you can't eat all the junk food you want. You can't watch all the TV you'd like. And unless you have a fever, you know you have to go to school *every* day."

I start to explain that all of these things are important because they are part of my birth month celebration, but Mom doesn't let me. She looks at my list again, and says my name slowly like she's talking to a two-year-old and not an almost nine-year-old.

"MAL-LOR-Y! We just painted your room. We're not going to repaint it. And your brother does not have to do all your chores for a month. How would you feel if you had to do all of Max's chores for a month?"

I wouldn't want to do that. I don't really want Max to have to do mine, but I don't think Mom understands that a celebration isn't a celebration unless you do something to celebrate it. I point to Way #7 on my list. "Can I get my ears pierced?"

Mom rubs the sides of her head, like she has a headache that won't go away.

"Mallory, we've talked about this. You can't get your ears pierced until you're twelve."

"But Mom! Getting my ears pierced is one of the most important ways I want to celebrate my birth month."

Mom shakes her head. "No pierced ears!" She hands the list to Dad.

He starts reading. "A gift of-the-day sounds like a nice idea." Dad rumples my hair. "How about a hug and a kiss . . . every day?"

"Not that kind of gift," I tell Dad.

"Sweet Potato," says Dad, "I've never heard of a month-long celebration that includes a gift a day."

"Let's talk about your party," says Mom.

"I know you've already planned my skating party," I say. "But what I really want is a surprise party."

"Mallory, you can't plan your own surprise party. If you do, you won't be surprised."

"I'll act surprised," I tell Mom. "Watch."

I stand up on the bed between Mom and Dad and put my hands on my cheeks. "I can't believe it!" I suck in air while I'm talking so I don't just look surprised. I sound surprised too. "All this for *me?*"

I look around the bedroom like I'm looking at friends and presents and decorations that I didn't expect to see. "I am just so, so, so surprised!"

Dad laughs. "Mallory, you are very good at acting surprised, but we've already planned your skating party."

"Turning nine is a big deal," I explain to Dad. "I want *everything* to be perfect."

"*Everything* will be great. We had a skating party for Max when he turned nine,

and it was a lot of fun."

I look down and pick a fuzz ball off the blanket. "I want this year to be better than last year, so it's important that it starts with the best-ever celebration. I've told you lots of ways I want to celebrate and you've said *no* to everything."

Mom looks at the list again. "Having Mary Ann visit is a nice idea. I'll call her mom and see if they can come down for your birthday weekend."

"I hope she can come." I look down and pick another fuzz ball off the blanket. "I can't imagine my birthday without my best friend."

"I'll call today," says Mom.

Dad clears his throat like he's a judge and he's about to say something important to the people in his courtroom. "Mallory, celebrations are nice. But whatever you do to celebrate your birthday won't affect the way your year turns out."

I know you're not supposed to argue with a judge, but I think Dad is wrong.

"Dad, it's like studying for a test," I say. "If you study, you make a good grade. If you plan a good celebration, you have a good year."

Dad pats me on the head, like he heard what I said but he doesn't agree. "I think we've had enough birthday talk for one morning. Why don't you go get dressed?"

I start to go downstairs. Then I stop.

"Wait a minute," I say. "What about Way #10? Celebrating each week of my birth month with a cake-of-the-week?"

Mom laughs. "A cake a week sounds like a sweet idea."

I can't believe Mom said *yes* to something. "Can we have a cake on Saturday?"

"I don't see why not," says Mom.

Now it's my turn to smile. "Can we have chocolate cake with fudge frosting and colored sprinkles?"

"Sounds like a plan," says Mom. "Now go get ready for school."

"OK," I tell Mom. But as I walk down the stairs, there's only one thing I can think about getting ready for, and that's my birth month celebration.

I've got a lot to do if it's going to be the best, best, best celebration ever.

MALLORY ON A MISSION

I'm on a mission. A *make-sure-everybody-knows-it's-my-birth-month* mission. There are a lot of people who I want to be part of my celebration. I split my mission into five parts.

MALLORY'S MISSION: PART I
Target: My brother, Max
Location: Our bathroom sink

When I walk into the bathroom, Max is already brushing his teeth. His dog, Champ, is with him.

I squirt toothpaste onto my toothbrush. "Guess what?" I say to Max. "I'm celebrating my birth month this year, not just my birth day. And today is the official start of my celebration."

Max spits into the sink. "Guess what? I'm skipping school and going fishing."

Sometimes Max says such dumb things.

"You can't skip school and go fishing."

"Well, you can't celebrate your birthday for a month." Max wipes off his mouth with the back of his hand.

"Give me three good reasons why not!"

Max rolls his eyes. "Because it's dumb. Because it's stupid. And because Mom and Dad won't let you."

I finish brushing and stick my toothbrush into my hole in the toothbrush holder.

"Mom already said I can have a cake a week during my birth month. I'm having my first cake on Saturday, and since you're my only brother, I want to make sure you'll be there to wish me *Happy Birth Month*."

I reach down and pet Champ. "He's invited too."

"Did you say you're having a cake a week for your birth month?"

I nod.

"And Mom agreed to that?"

I nod again. "Max, I'm turning nine. This is a very important celebration."

Max rolls his eyes. "I'm turning eleven, and you don't see me celebrating my birthday for a month. And the last time I checked, nine was no big deal."

Max might not think nine is a big deal now, but he will on Saturday when he has a big piece of chocolate cake on his plate.

Part I of my mission is complete. On to Part II.

MALLORY'S MISSION: PART II
   Target: My next-door neighbors, Joey and
               Winnie Winston
   Location: On our way to school

"knock, knock," I say as we walk toward

Elementary.

"'s there?" asks Joey.

"Itzmy," I say smiling.

"Itzmy?" Winnie repeats the name like it's the title of a boring book she has to read for school and not the first part of a

knock-knock joke.

Joey ignores his sister. "Itzmy who?" he asks.

"It's my birth month celebration starting today," I tell them. "I'm having a cake a week. My first one is on Saturday, and you're both invited."

Winnie's lip curls up like a sleeping bag. "Who ever heard of celebrating a birth month? Count me out. I've got more important things to do, like brush my hair." Winnie walks ahead of Joey and me.

I look at Joey. "Can you come on Saturday?"

"I don't know," he says. "I'm supposed to go ice skating with Pete on Saturday."

"C'mon! I'll make sure you get an extra-big piece."

Joey's been a great friend ever since I moved to Fern Falls. I know he'll be there.

Part II of my mission is complete. Now, it's time for Part III.

MALLORY'S MISSION: PART III
 Target: My desk mate, Pamela
 Location: Fern Falls Elementary, Room 310
 As soon as I walk into my classroom, Mrs. Daily tells us to open our science books to page ninety-six. "Today, we're starting our unit on astronauts and space," she says.

 I open up my science book and turn the pages slowly. It's not that I mind learning about astronauts and space, but what I really want to do is invite Pamela to my birth month celebration.

 I just don't want to celebrate without her.

 Mrs. Daily starts reading about rockets. I start a note to my desk mate.

Pamela,

I am celebrating my birth month, which starts TODAY!!!!!!

Can you come to a celebration at my house on Saturday?

Hugs, Mallory

I fold my note into a tiny square and pass it to Pamela. When she's done reading, she turns it over and writes something on the back, then refolds the piece of paper and passes it back to me.

Mallory,

Happy birth month!

I would love to help you celebrate, but I have a violin lesson on Saturday.

I have to talk to my mom.

Hugs back, Pamela

When I finish reading, I smile at Pamela.
"*See you Saturday*," I mouth to her.

I know Pamela's mom will let her come
to my house. Everyone knows a birth
month celebration is a lot more important
than a violin lesson.

Part III of my mission is complete. On to
Part IV.

MALLORY'S MISSION: PART IV

Target: Grandma

Location: On the phone

When I get home from school, I don't even stop for a snack. I go straight to the phone and dial Grandma's number.

When she answers, I tell her right away about the special celebration I have planned. "Grandma, I decided to celebrate my birth month this year!"

And before Grandma has a chance to say anything, my birth month plans start spilling out of my mouth like chocolate chips falling from an open bag. "I'm having a cake a week, and Mary Ann might come to visit, and I'm having a party!" I tell her.

"Slow down," says Grandma.

But once I get started, it's hard to slow down. "Even though I really wanted to have a surprise party, I'm having a skating party. And I know you live a long way away, but I wanted to know if you can come to my party."

Grandma sighs into the phone. "Honey Bee, I do live a long way away, but I'm planning to send you something special for your birthday this year."

I smile into the phone. "Can you give me a hint about what you're sending?"

Grandma laughs. "No hints. But I think you'll like it."

Knowing Grandma, I'm sure I will. I tell Grandma good-bye, then I head to my room. There's still one very important person that needs to know about my birth month celebration.

MALLORY'S MISSION: PART V
Target: My best, best, best friend, Mary Ann
Location: My desk in my room

Dear Mary Ann,

I have something important to tell you. I'm celebrating my birth month this year!

I know that's not something we've done before, but I decided to do things differently this year.

If you're wondering why, I'll tell you.

Being eight was my worst, worst, worst year ever!!! If I had to rate it, I'd give it a big thumbs-down. (Moving and leaving you was the worst part!)

I want to make nine the best year ever, so I'm planning to start it off with the best-ever celebration!

Even though Mom said no to lots of ways that I want to celebrate, like getting my ears pierced (she said I have to wait until I'm twelve) and having a surprise party (she already planned a skating party), she said yes to you coming to visit on my birthday!

I hope your mom says you can come!

WRITE ME AS SOON AS YOU KNOW IF YOU ARE COMING!

Biggest, hugest hugs and kisses ever,
Mallory

P.S. Here's something Mom said yes to: a cake-a-week for my birth month! This Saturday I'm having my first cake, chocolate with sprinkles! It will be great except for one thing: NO YOU! BOO-HOO!

I finish my letter and stick it in an envelope. Max, Joey, Winnie, Pamela,

Grandma, and Mary Ann all know about
my special celebration. Now I feel like my
birth month can begin. I put my hands
behind my head and my feet on my desk,
like I've seen detectives do on TV when
they crack a case.

"Cheeseburger," I say to my cat,
"mission accomplished."

SADDER DAY

"AH-CHOO!"

That makes sixty-seven times Mom has sneezed since she woke up this morning. I walk into the den with a box of tissues.

"AH-CHOO!"

Sixty-eight.

I hand Mom the box.

Mom looks at me. At least she tries to look at me, but her eyes are all puffy and swollen from coughing and sneezing.

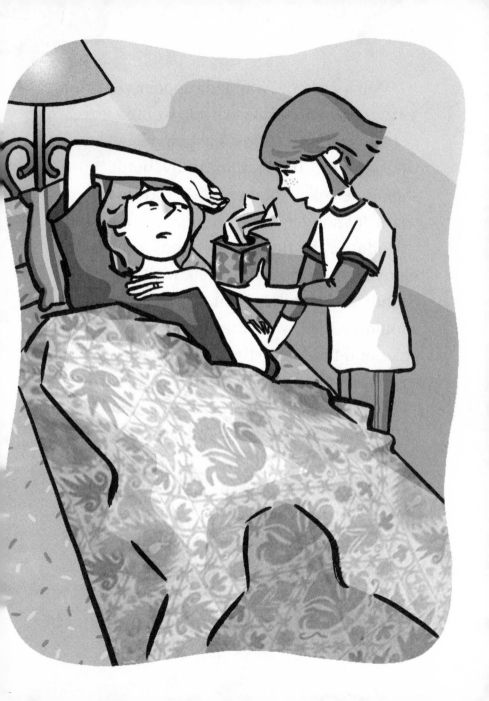

"Mallory, I know you're disappointed. I'm sorry today isn't going like you wanted it to."

Mom is right. Today *isn't* going like I wanted it to. Today is Saturday, but it should be called "*Sadder Day.*" Today is a whole lot sadder than I thought it would be.

Today is the day I was supposed to be enjoying a cake-of-the-week with my friends and family. Right now, my mouth should be filled with the taste of chocolate cake and fudge frosting. But right now, my mouth is empty.

"Don't look so glum," says Dad. He walks into the den and hands me an envelope with my name on it. "The postman paid you a visit."

I take my envelope, walk into the kitchen, and sit down at the table.

I didn't get a cake-of-the-week, but at least I get a letter from my best friend.

Dear Mallory,

Happy, happy, happy birth month!!!!!!

Are you having the best birth month ever? I bet you are.

I have some very happy birth month news that I know you will like hearing.

I'M COMING TO VISIT! Did your mom tell you yet? My mom said we can come for your whole birth weekend! (I figured there must be such a thing as a birth weekend since there is such a thing as a birth month.)

I wanted to come for the whole month. Mom said no to that, but she did say I will be there for your skating party! I am so, so, so excited! I don't think it matters that you're not having a surprise party. Skating parties are fun, too!

See you soon, soon, soon!

Hugs and kisses,

Mary Ann

P.S. How was your cake-of-the-week? I want to hear about it, down to the very last sprinkle.

P.P.S. I hope you took pictures when you blew out your candles. When I come visit, we can make a birth month scrapbook.

P.P.P.S. Tell your mom that nine is OLD to get your ears pierced. I got mine pierced when I was eight. Remember? Maybe you should try asking your mom in a different way. I just know she'll say yes!

I reread the letter from Mary Ann. Then I take a sheet of paper from Mom's desk and start writing.

Dear Mary Ann,

I have some bad, bad, bad news.

My birth month isn't going like I had planned.

It's a long, sad story. But since you're my best friend, I'll tell it to you anyway.

I didn't get a cake-of-the-week because Mom didn't bake a cake-of-the-week because she has the flu.

Even if she had baked it, no one would have come to eat it, because Joey had other plans and Pamela had violin lessons and Max and Winnie both said it was dumb.

Since I didn't have a cake, I don't have any pictures to put in my birth month scrapbook.

I hope this story did not make you too sad. I am counting the days and minutes and seconds until you get here.

Mallory

P.S. Mom hasn't said yes to getting my ears pierced yet, but I think she will. (See plan below for how I'm going to ask her.)

I finish my letter to Mary Ann, fold it, and stick it in the envelope.

The first week of my birth month wasn't so great. I try not to think about what *didn't* happen and instead think about all the good things that are *going* to happen.

I think about the cake-of-the-week I'm going to have next week. I think about the class party I'm going to have the week after that. I think about Mary Ann coming to visit. Then, I think about how much fun it will be to have pierced ears.

I reach up and feel the soft, floppy part of my earlobes.

Tonight . . . I will put Operation Earrings into action.

Tomorrow . . . there will be holes where today there were none.

THE HOLE STORY

"Good morning, class," says Mrs. Daily. "How was everyone's weekend?"

Room 310 fills up with *goods* and *greats* and *supers* and *terrifics*. There are even a few *amazings*. But I'm quiet. I wouldn't describe the first weekend of my birth month as good or great or super or terrific, and definitely not amazing.

"What did everyone do?" asks Mrs. Daily.

"I went ice skating," says Joey.

"Me too," says Pete.

"I took a violin lesson," calls out Pamela.

"We went shopping," says Danielle.

"Shoe shopping," says Arielle.

Both girls stick their feet in the air to show the class their matching sneakers.

Mrs. Daily smiles at Danielle and Arielle's feet.

Then she smiles at me. "Mallory, what did you do this weekend?"

All I can think about is what I *didn't* do. "Nothing," I mumble.

"Well, I'm sure you did something," says Mrs. Daily. She picks up a piece of chalk and writes *What I Did This Weekend* on the chalkboard.

"Class, this morning, I'd like you all to write a one-page essay on what you did

this weekend. Use details about what
happened to make the reader feel like they
were there with you."

Everyone takes out paper and pencils,
but not me. I don't get out anything to
write with because I don't have anything to
write about. Mrs. Daily comes over to my
desk. "Having trouble getting started?"

I nod.

"Think for a minute," says Mrs. Daily.
"You'll come up with something."

"I know what Mallory can write about,"
says Pamela. "She's turning nine soon.
She can write about what she did this
weekend to celebrate her birthday."

Pamela winks at me like she knows what
I did this weekend. But what Pamela
doesn't know is that I didn't do anything.

Mrs. Daily clears her throat. "Mallory, what do you think of that idea?"

I think about my weekend. I didn't get a cake. I tried to talk to Mom about getting my ears pierced. But that didn't work either.

"Mrs. Daily, would it be OK if I write about what I *didn't* do this weekend?"

Mrs. Daily says if that's what I remember

about my weekend, then I can certainly write about it. I take out a sheet of paper and begin.

The Hole Story
By Mallory McDonald
Author's Note: You will need tissues when you read this story. It is very sad!

Once upon a time, there was a little girl who was about to turn nine. All she wanted for her birthday were two little holes, one in each ear. So one weekend, she asked her mother if she could get these two little holes.

Her mother said, "NO! You may not have two little holes, one in each ear, until you turn twelve."

So the little girl did what any other

little girl who was about to turn nine (and wanted something really, really, really badly) would do.

She begged and pleaded with her mother.

Her mother still said, "NO!"

So then, the little girl scrubbed the floor. That was how she spent her weekend. SCRUBBING THE FLOOR! She hoped this would get her mother to change her mind.

But guess what? It didn't work. Her mother still said, "NO!" (This was mean and cruel of her mother, don't you think?)

So the little girl offered to pay for the holes in her ears with her very own allowance money and eat spinach if her mother would just let her get those two tiny, little holes. But her mother still said, "NO!"

The little girl was starting to think things were hopeless. But she didn't give up.

She told her mother that the only thing she would need to make her birth month (which hadn't been so great so far) extra-special would be those two little holes.

You won't believe what happened next.

You will never EVER guess.

Her mother still said, "NO!" And, to top it off, she sent the girl to her room for not listening the first time.

When that happened, a tear ran down the girl's cheek. She had no choice but to wipe it away and move on with her life.

The moral of the story is that mothers should not say no to their children because it makes them very sad.

The End

When I finish my story, I look at my desk mate. Pamela is still busy writing. I put my head down on my desk. I knew my birth month wasn't going so well, but I didn't realize how bad it was until now.

I close my eyes and do what I do when I

want something to happen and I'm not sure it's going to. I pretend like I'm at the wish pond on my street, and I make a wish.

I wish that the second week of my birth month will be better than the first week.

I try to draw a picture in my brain of the cookie cake with rainbow writing that I want for my second cake-of-the-week. When I know exactly what it looks like, I pretend to throw a wish pebble in the wish pond.

I sure hope my wish comes true.

HALF-
BIRTHDAYS

Grandma says when you're waiting for something to happen, time goes slowly. She says there's a clock fairy that sits on the hands of the clock to slow them down.

The clock fairy must have been sitting on my clock because this week felt like the slowest week of my life. I never thought today would get here.

I sit up in bed and look at my calendar. "Cheeseburger," I say to my cat, "this Saturday is going to be different than last Saturday."

Last Saturday, I was sad, sad, sad. Just thinking about the chocolate cake with fudge frosting that I didn't get makes me feel like staying in bed. But this Saturday, I'm happy, happy, happy. I'm celebrating my birth month with a cookie cake with rainbow writing!

I scoop up Cheeseburger, pop out of bed, and skip into the bathroom.

I open up my hair-thingies drawer and pull out my rainbow ribbon. I put my hair in a ponytail and tie the ribbon around it. When I'm finished, I look in the mirror. "My hair will match the icing on my cookie cake," I tell Cheeseburger.

I tuck her under my arm and skip down

the hall into the kitchen.

Mom smiles when she sees me. "Mallory, I'm glad it's you. Would you like to help me bake a cake?"

Someone should give Mom a T-shirt that says *Mind Reader.*

"That's exactly what I'd like to do!"

"I was hoping you'd say that," says Mom. She opens up her cookbook and starts taking ingredients from the pantry. Flour, sugar, vanilla, coconut.

I pick up the bag of coconut. I love cookie cake, but I hate coconut. I'm surprised cookie cake has something in it that I hate.

I look at the recipe in Mom's cookbook, and when I do, I get another surprise. "Mom, this isn't a recipe for cookie cake. This is a recipe for coconut cake."

Mom takes eggs and butter from the

refrigerator.

"You know I don't like coconut, so why would you bake a coconut cake for my cake-of-the-week?" I say to Mom.

"Mallory, this cake is for Winnie," says Mom. "We're invited to the Winstons' tonight to celebrate her half-birthday. Mr. Winston asked if I would bake a cake."

This cake wasn't supposed to be for

Winnie! "Mom, why are we celebrating Winnie's birthday, which is half a year away, when my birthday is in less than two weeks?"

Mom puts the eggs and butter down on the counter. "Winnie will be at sleepaway camp on her real birthday, so she wants to celebrate her half-birthday at home."

"Why don't we make two cakes?" I say to Mom. "We can celebrate Winnie's half-birthday and my birth month."

Max walks into the kitchen and grabs a banana. "Enough with the birth month stuff," he says. "It's getting stupid."

I put my hands on my hips. "If you think celebrating my birth month is stupid, I bet you think celebrating Winnie's half-birthday is really stupid."

Max takes a bite of banana. "That's different."

I don't see what's different about it. I march over to where Mom is mixing. "You said I could have a cake-a-week for my birth month, remember?"

Mom stops mixing. "Mallory, I never said you could have a cake-a-week."

"You said it was a sweet idea."

Mom takes a deep breath. She says my name slowly like she has something to tell me and she isn't sure where to start. "Mal-lor-y, I think we've had a misunderstanding. Having a cake is always a fun thing to do, but I didn't mean you could have one every week."

"Can I have one tonight?"

"Tonight is Winnie's night. We're going to the Winstons' house for her celebration." She drops a stick of butter into the mixer. Then she continues talking. "You have a lot to look forward to. Next Friday is your class party. Then, Mary Ann and her mom are coming to visit. And, you're having a skating party."

I start to explain to Mom why she's not being fair, but she gives me a *that's-the-end-of-this-discussion* look. She pours a cup of sugar into the mixer and turns it on.

I go into my room and sit down on my bed with Cheeseburger.

I think about my birth month. It isn't going the way I wanted it to. Just thinking about it gives me a funny feeling . . . and that feeling stays with me all day. I still have it as we walk next door to the Winstons' for Winnie's half-birthday party.

"Welcome," Mr. Winston says to Mom, Dad, Max, and me when he answers the door. "What a beautiful cake," he says to Mom when he sees what she's holding.

I look at the words *Happy Half-Birthday,*

Winnie on the top of the cake. I can't help wishing they said *Happy Birth Month, Mallory.*

Mr. Winston pats me on the head. "Joey's in his room. Why don't you go get him and come to the kitchen. Then the party can start."

I walk down the hall to Joey's room. His

door is open, so I walk in. "Ready for Winnie's party?"

"Yeah," Joey says. Then he points to a calendar on his wall. "I'm ready for your party too. Just one week and two days till we go skating."

I shrug my shoulders.

"Aren't you excited?"

I don't want Joey to think I'm unexcited to have a party, so I explain. "The thing is, I really didn't want a skating party. I don't even have my own skates."

"You can rent skates at the skating rink," says Joey. He smiles like he has all the answers. "See, no problem."

Joey says "no problem" like my birthday is going to be great. But the thing is, I don't feel like it's going to be great. I don't feel like anything is going the way I wanted it to.

When we walk into the kitchen, balloons and streamers are hanging from the ceiling. There's a sign on the wall that says *Happy Half-Birthday, Winnie!* Two big boxes wrapped in yellow tissue paper are sitting on the counter.

"We have everything Winnie likes tonight. Pizza, spaghetti, and Caesar salad," says Mr. Winston.

Joey points to the boxes on the counter. "Presents too."

Winnie smiles like she's really happy. Usually, she only smiles if somebody else did something dumb. "Dad," she says, "can I open my presents now?"

Mr. Winston laughs. "How about after dinner?"

Everybody takes plates and piles them high with pizza, spaghetti, and salad. I love pizza, spaghetti, and salad, but tonight, I

put just a little of each on my plate.

Joey looks at the single strand of spaghetti on my plate. "Mallory, is that all you want? I thought spaghetti was one of your favorites."

I look down at my plate. "I'm not very hungry."

Joey pretends to feel my forehead. "You're not getting sick are you?"

Joey is not a doctor. I shake my head *no* and move his hand.

"Pre-birthday jitters?" he asks.

I know Joey is trying to be funny and make me laugh. But I don't. I shake my head *no* again.

Mr. Winston looks concerned. "Mallory, is something bothering you?"

I wasn't going to bring this up, but since he asked, I explain. "It's just that tonight, I was supposed to . . . "

Before I can even say the words *celebrate my birth month*, Dad stops me.

"Everything is fine," says Dad. He gives me a *stop-talking-and-start-eating* look. Mom looks at me too, like she can't believe what I was about to say.

I stick my fork into a piece of lettuce and chew my Caesar salad in silence. I feel like nobody, not even Mom and Dad, cares about celebrating my birth month.

After dinner, we sing *Happy Half-Birthday* to Winnie. Even Max, who never sings, sings. Winnie blows out her candles, then she opens her presents.

She gets a new sweater from her dad and a matching hat and gloves from Joey.

She pulls her hat on her head to model it. "I love everything!" says Winnie.

Everyone is smiling.

I try to smile too, but my mouth is

having a hard time cooperating.

"Can we cut the cake now?" asks Winnie.

Mom slices and Joey passes around plates.

I look at Mom. She gives me a slice of coconut cake and a *don't-be-rude* look.

I think about the piece of cookie cake that should be on this plate, and even though I hate coconut cake, I do something I never thought I was going to have to do during my birth month . . . I take a bite.

There's only one thing worse than a birth month that isn't going like you wanted it to . . . and that's a mouthful of coconut.

PARTY POOPED

"MOM! DAD! COME QUICK!" I yell from my bedroom.

I hear Mom and Dad running down the hall. They're in my bedroom in less time than it takes to sneeze.

"Mallory, what's the matter?" asks Dad. He's out of breath.

I hold up a purple turtleneck with fringe and a pink sweater covered in hearts. "Which one do you think I should wear?"

Mom and Dad look at each other, then Dad puts his hands over his heart. "Phew!" he says. "I thought something was wrong."

I put my hands on my hips. "Something is wrong! I can't decide which outfit to wear for my class party today. I don't want to pick the wrong one!"

Mom smiles. "I'm glad to see you're so excited."

I look in the mirror and hold my two outfits up to my face. Then I smile at Mom.

"Of course I'm excited! I just don't know how I'm going to be able to wait until you and Dad get to my classroom this afternoon with the cupcakes."

Dad laughs. "Visions of pink cupcakes will be dancing through your head."

"That's it!" I tell Dad. "You just gave me a great idea!" I stick the purple turtleneck back into my drawer and pull the pink sweater over my head. Then I pull on the matching pink pants. "I'll wear pink, so I match my cupcakes."

"Glad I could help," says Dad. He kisses my forehead. "I've got to go to work, but I'll see you this afternoon."

Mom ruffles my hair. "Hurry," she says. "You don't want to be late for school."

Mom is right. I don't want to miss a minute of what I know will be the best day yet of my birth month.

I go into my bathroom. I tie a big pink bow in my hair and pull a handful of pink stretchy bracelets over my wrist. "Now I'm perfectly pink!" I tell Cheeseburger. I pick up my cat and walk into the kitchen.

Max is already at the breakfast table with Champ. When I walk in, he looks up and laughs. "Did you fall into a bucket of pink paint?"

I take a waffle out of the toaster and sit down at the breakfast table. "For your information, I picked pink on purpose."

Max looks at me like that makes about as much sense as choosing a day-old doughnut. "Why would anybody pick pink on purpose?"

I think about the vanilla cupcakes with strawberry icing that Dad is picking up from the bakery this afternoon. "My class party is today, and I'm wearing pink so I'll match my cupcakes," I tell Max.

Max laughs, and when he does, little bits of waffle fly out of his mouth and land on his plate. "I've heard of eating cupcakes, but I've never heard of matching them."

Champ licks Max's plate.

Mom passes Max a napkin. "Today is a special day for Mallory."

Mom is right. Today is special, and I don't want anything to go wrong. "Can we go over the plan again?" I ask.

Mom nods.

"Dad is picking up the cupcakes from the bakery this afternoon?"

Mom nods again.

"And you're bringing everything else?"

"I've got it all," says Mom. "Don't worry."

But I can't help worrying. So far, my birth month hasn't gone like I had planned, and I don't want anything to mess up my

class party. "Can we check the bag one more time?"

Mom opens the grocery bag with all the party supplies in it. Candles. Matches. *Happy Birthday* plates and napkins. Mom's camera, so she can take pictures for my birth month scrapbook.

"Everything we need to make sure today is the best-school-party-ever is in the bag," Mom says.

On the way to school, I tell Joey how

excited I am. "I don't know how I'm going to be able to wait all day," I say as we walk into Room 310.

Joey looks at his watch. "You actually only have to wait six hours."

Maybe six hours isn't all day, but to me, it feels like it might as well be six years. I can't wait until this afternoon!

Before Mrs. Daily makes everyone sit down, I tell my friends that my parents are bringing birthday cupcakes at the end of the day.

"Oooh, I love cupcakes," squeals Danielle.

"Me too," says Arielle.

"What kind are they?" asks Pamela.

"The yummy kind," I tell Pamela. I want everyone to be surprised when they see my cupcakes.

"Class, please take your seats," says Mrs. Daily. "We have a lot to do today, and we have a birthday party at the end of the day." Mrs. Daily smiles at me, then she writes *Happy Birthday, Mallory* on the chalkboard.

"Mallory's real birthday is on Monday, but since there's no school on Monday, we're going to celebrate today."

Mrs. Daily tells us to open our math books to page 112.

During math, I try to focus on multiplication, but I keep looking at the clock.

Every time I do, the hands remind me of candles, and I think about my class party at the end of the day.

Some school days go by slowly, but today is the slowest ever.

I can hardly wait for 2:30 to get here.

When it finally does, I stop watching the clock and start watching the door. "My parents should be here any minute," I tell Pamela.

"Soon it will be lights, camera, cupcakes!" she says.

I watch the door swing open, and Mom walks in. She walks over to my desk and hugs me. "You have everything," I say looking into the grocery bag in her arms.

"Almost everything," she says smiling. "Dad should be here any minute with the cupcakes."

The door swings open again and Dad walks in. But his hands are empty. "Where are the cupcakes?" I ask when he comes over to my desk.

Dad pats me on the head. "Sweetheart, Mom has the cupcakes."

I look at Dad. "She said *you* were bringing them."

Dad looks at Mom. "Sherry, you have the cupcakes, right?"

Mom shakes her head. "Harry, you were supposed to stop at the bakery on the way here and pick them up."

"I thought you were bringing everything," says Dad. Mom and Dad start whispering to each other.

If they are playing a birthday joke on me, it's not funny. "Who brought the cupcakes?" I ask softly. I know somebody has to have the cupcakes, because you can't have a party without them.

Dad puts his hands on my shoulders. He has a funny look on his face. "Sweet Potato, I'm afraid Mom and I had a little mix-up."

"Is there a problem?" Mrs. Daily asks.

Mom explains to Mrs. Daily that Dad was supposed to pick up the cupcakes, but he thought she was bringing them.

"You mean no one brought the cupcakes?!?" I say.

Mom and Dad don't say anything, but I know the answer. There are no lights. There are no cameras. THERE ARE NO CUPCAKES!

"Can't Dad go get them?" I ask.

Mrs. Daily looks at me. "Mallory, school ends soon. There's not enough time for your dad to go get the cupcakes and bring them back in time to have a party."

"I've got some mints in my purse," says Mom. "Why don't I pass out mints to everyone, and we can still sing *Happy Birthday?*"

I sit down at my desk. "You can't put a candle in a mint," I say to Mom.

"I've got some potato chips," says Joey.

"You can't stick a candle in a chip, either," I tell him.

"How about half a tuna sandwich from my lunch?" says Pamela. "We could stick a candle in that."

I look down at the floor. I don't want everyone to sing *Happy Birthday* to me over mints or potato chips or tuna fish. I want my pink and white cupcakes.

Mrs. Daily puts her arm around me. "We don't need cupcakes to celebrate your birthday. Class, let's all sing *Happy Birthday* to Mallory."

I try to smile while my class sings. But inside, I don't feel very smiley.

Dad puts his arm around me. "Mallory, Mom and I made a mistake, and we sure are sorry." He hugs me. "I feel like a real party pooper," says Dad.

"Me too," says Mom.

Me three. I feel like my party pooped before it ever popped.

Joey comes over to me. "Hey, at least Mary Ann will be here tonight."

I try to smile. I know Mom and Dad didn't mean to forget the cupcakes. And I know Joey is trying to make me feel better, but so far, my birth month celebration has been a big, fat flop.

At least Joey's right about one thing: Mary Ann is coming tonight. And when she gets here, I just know everything will get better.

It can't get worse.

MALLORY GETS A MAKEOVER

I line up bottles and jars, brushes and combs on my bathroom sink. Then I look at my watch. "Cheeseburger," I say, "we've got a lot to do, and not much time to do it."

Mary Ann and her mom will be here in less than an hour. The Winstons are coming over for a pre-birthday dinner.

Tonight is the official start of my birth weekend. And it's not just a regular birth weekend. There's no school on Monday, so it's a three-day-long birth weekend.

Even though my class party was a flop, I know tonight will be great. And I want to look great. I want to look like I'm turning nine on Monday because on Monday . . . I AM TURNING NINE!!!

I look at Cheeseburger. "Why don't we start with makeup." Mom usually won't let me wear makeup, but she said I could put on a little since tonight is a special occasion.

I brush sparkly peach blush on my cheeks. I coat my lips with shiny pink lip gloss. I even put a dab of shimmery blue shadow on my eyelids. Then I paint my nails with pale yellow polish and blow on them, so they'll dry quickly.

"How do I look?" I ask Cheeseburger.

She purrs. I take that as a good sign. "Now it's time for hair," I say.

I open up my drawer with all my hair thingies in it. I take out a pair of barrettes. I pull back a little hair on each side of my face and clip in the barrettes.

I look in the mirror. This doesn't look like a nine-year-old hairstyle. I rip out the barrettes and pull my hair into a ponytail on top of my head.

But when I look in the mirror, I don't like what I see. "This doesn't even look like an eight-year-old hairstyle," I mumble to Cheeseburger.

I take out the ponytail, fluff up my

bangs, and put a little gel on the ends. I even try twisting the ends into little curls. I still don't like what I see.

"Cheeseburger, what I need is a nine-year-old makeover. Any ideas?" But when I look at Cheeseburger, she's asleep on top of the toilet.

I try rubbing my forehead with my pinkies. That's what I always do when I'm trying to think of a good idea. But today, it's not so easy to rub my forehead with my pinkies, because my forehead is covered up with bangs.

I try pushing them to the side, but they fall back down onto my face.

And that's when I get an idea. NOT being able to rub my forehead gives me a great idea. What I need is less hair on my forehead. I stare into the mirror and try to imagine what I would look like if my bangs weren't so long.

What I imagine is me, but not eight-year-old me. I see nine-year-old Mallory. I walk over to my desk and get my scissors. "I'm just going to cut a little off the bottom," I say to Cheeseburger when I'm back in the bathroom.

I start on the left side of my forehead and work my way to the right. When I'm finished, I look in the mirror. The left side looks a little longer than the right side.

I cut a little more off the left, just to even it up. But when I'm done, the left side looks a little shorter to me than the right side.

Cutting bangs isn't as easy as I thought it would be.

I nudge Cheeseburger so she'll wake up.

She opens her eyes. "Cheeseburger, I need a second opinion." I point to the right side of my bangs. "Does this side look a

little shorter to you?"

Cheeseburger purrs. I take that as a *yes*.
I snip some hair off the bottom of the right
side of my bangs.

Now the right side looks MUCH shorter
than the left, and I don't need a second
opinion to know that.

I pull the left side of my bangs into a
chunk and start snipping.

When I'm finished, I look in the mirror.

What I would like to see are bangs that are even on the left side and the right side. But what I see are NO bangs on the left side.

"CHEESEBURGER!" I scream. "LOOK AT MY HAIR!"

Cheeseburger jumps when I scream, and she looks at me. I can tell by the way she's looking that she thinks something is wrong.

I can't have bangs on one side and not the other. I grab the scissors and snip off the bangs on the right side of my forehead to try to make things even.

When I'm finished, I look in the mirror. Now I have NO bangs on either side! I don't look like *nine-year-old* Mallory. I look like a Ping-Pong ball. I reach up to feel the spot where my bangs used to be. It feels prickly.

"This is awful!" I tell Cheeseburger. I can't believe I cut my bangs off . . . right when Mary Ann is coming to town, right

before my birthday.

I can feel my eyes filling up with tears.

"Oh, Cheeseburger!" I moan. "What am I going to do?"

But Cheeseburger just stares at the pile of hair on the floor that used to be my bangs.

"Mary Ann is going to be here any minute. I don't want anyone to see me like this, not even my best friend," I tell Cheeseburger. Tears roll down my cheeks.

There's only one thing I can do. I go into my bedroom and lock the door.

I'm staying in my room forever . . . or at least until my bangs grow out. I try to think how long it will take.

One time when I got a haircut, the haircutter told me that hair grows one-half an inch a month. I try to measure my forehead with my index finger. It's about two inches long, which means I'll be stuck in my room for at least four months.

If I'm stuck in here for that long, I could starve! I'm hungry already.

"Mallory!" Mom yells from the kitchen. "Mary Ann is here."

I pull aside my curtains and look outside. Mary Ann's mom's van is in the driveway. I see the Winstons walking over. I close my curtains. I don't want any of them to see me.

I hear everyone inside my house.

"Mallory!" Mom calls my name again.

I hear footsteps running down the hall.

"Mallory! Open up! I'm here! " says a familiar voice on the other side of my door.

I reach up and rub my prickly spot. I can't let Mary Ann see me like this.

"Mallory? Are you in there?"

I don't answer. I hear Mary Ann going

back down the hall.

Then I hear more footsteps and voices coming toward my room. "Mallory, open up."

"I can't come out," I tell Dad.

"Why not?" Dad sounds concerned.

"I can't tell you why, but trust me, I can't."

"She has to come out," Mary Ann says to Dad.

"C'mon," says Dad. "Everyone's here. Mary Ann, Joey, Winnie. It's time for your pre-birthday dinner."

"I'm not coming out," I tell Dad. "Not now. Not for a long time."

"Mallory," says Dad. "I'm going to count to three, and I want you to open this door."

Dad counts, but I don't open the door.

"Mallory Louise McDonald, open this door this instant!" says Dad.

I don't.

"I think your dad went to get your mom," says Mary Ann.

She's right. Mom is at my door in less time than it takes to cut off your bangs. "Mallory, what's wrong? You need to come out of your room. We want to start dinner, and we can't start without you."

I don't answer Mom. I just curl up on my bed next to Cheeseburger.

"Mallory, I'm not going to ask again. You need to come out of your room now, and if you don't, we're starting without you."

I think about the cheeseburgers Dad is making on the grill. I think about the cupcakes and ice cream Mom is serving for dessert. I think about how much fun it would be to celebrate my birthday with my family and friends.

Then I think about my hair. I can just hear what Max would say if he saw me

without bangs. *If you look up the word ugly in the dictionary, you'd see Mallory's picture next to it.*

"Start without me," I tell Mom.

I pull Cheeseburger close to me. "It's just you and me," I tell her, "for the next four months."

A PAJAMA PARTY

Mary Ann bangs on my door. "C'mon," she says. "Open up. I've been here for two hours, and I haven't even seen you yet."

I want to see my best friend, but I don't want her to see me. "I'm not opening my door," I tell Mary Ann.

"Why not?" she asks.

"I can't tell you why not."

"But I'm your best friend," says Mary Ann. "You can tell me anything. We came here to celebrate your birthday, and I can't celebrate if I can't see you!"

"Mallory, open up right now," says Dad. I watch my doorknob rattle.

I know I can't stay locked in my room forever. Mary Ann is my best friend, and she did come to celebrate my birthday. I take my snow hat out of the closet and pull it down over my forehead. I open my door.

When I do, Mom, Dad, Max, Mary Ann, and her mom are all standing there.

They walk into my room. "What's going on?" asks Mom. She looks suspicious.

Mary Ann gives me a hug. "Your pre-birthday dinner wasn't much fun without you." Then she gets a funny look on her face. "Why are you wearing your hat inside?"

Before I can stop her, Mary Ann reaches up and pulls my hat off my head.

"MALLORY?" Mom says my name like she's not sure she recognizes me.

Mary Ann puts her hands on her cheeks. "Mallory, where are your bangs?"

I cover my forehead with one hand and

point toward my bathroom with the other. "On the floor in there," I say.

Max laughs. "I never thought I'd say this, but they looked better on than off."

"Max, that's enough." Mom gives Max a sharp look. Then she walks over to me and inspects what's left of my hair. "Honey, why did you cut your bangs?" Mom asks.

I explain that my makeover didn't turn out like I thought it would. When I'm finished talking, Mom puts her arm around me. "It's really not a big deal. Your hair will grow back before you know it."

Dad smiles at me. "Just think of all the money we'll save on shampoo."

I know Dad is trying to make me laugh, but I'm not in the mood for jokes.

"I think you look cute and grown up." Mary Ann's mom puts one arm around me and the other around Mary Ann. "Now why don't we get out of here and let you two catch up with each other."

I might have lost my bangs, but at least I still have my best friend. "That sounds great," I say.

After everyone leaves, I look at Mary Ann. "What am I going to do?"

"We're going to find a new hairstyle for you," says Mary Ann.

"Do you really think we can?"

Mary Ann nods. "Of course we can!"

I hug her. "You're the best, best, best friend in the whole wide world."

Mary Ann grins. "Let's put on our pajamas first, and we'll have a *Find-a-New-Hairstyle-for-Mallory* pajama party."

Now it's my turn to grin. Mary Ann knows I love pajama parties!

Mary Ann pulls her penguin pajamas out of her suitcase. I put on my matching ones, then scoop up Cheeseburger and follow Mary Ann into the bathroom.

She opens my hair-thingies drawer and pulls out handfuls of ribbons, headbands, and clips. "We're going to have to experiment until we find the right hairstyle for you." Mary Ann picks up a purple ribbon and ties it into a big bow on the front of my head.

I look in the mirror, but when I see myself, I shut my eyes. "I look like an overgrown baby," I tell Mary Ann.

Mary Ann looks at my reflection in the mirror, then unties the bow. I open one eye and watch while she pins in butterfly clips all over the front of my head.

"What do you think?" asks Mary Ann.

I look in the mirror. "I think I look like the butterfly exhibit at the zoo."

"Hmmm," says Mary Ann. "I see what you mean." She takes the clips out. "Let's try this." She pushes a thick striped headband over the front of my head.

I look in the mirror and smile. "I like it!"

Cheeseburger purrs. "I think Cheeseburger likes it too," says Mary Ann. She smiles. "You look cute with or without bangs," she says.

When I cut off my bangs, I thought tonight would be a total disaster, but it turned out OK. I throw my arms around Mary Ann. "This has been our best pajama party ever."

Mary Ann nods, like she agrees.

"We'll have to go headband shopping," I say to Mary Ann. I start thinking about all my different outfits. "I'll need a red one and a purple one and a green one and a blue one. Maybe we'll go tomorrow," I say.

Mary Ann grins. "I can't believe I forgot to tell you what's happening tomorrow."

I try to think what could be happening tomorrow. Tomorrow is Saturday. My skating party isn't until Monday. Maybe Mom planned something else on Saturday for my birth month celebration.

"Are you sure it's OK to tell me?" I ask Mary Ann. "I wouldn't want to spoil any surprises."

Mary Ann smiles even bigger than when she found the perfect hairstyle for me. "I think you'll be surprised when you hear this. Tonight at dinner, my mom and Joey's dad sat next to each other."

I shrug my shoulders. "What's the big deal about them sitting next to each other?"

"I think they liked sitting next to each other, because tomorrow night, they're going out on a date. Isn't that great?" squeals Mary Ann.

I rub my ear. "I guess so," I say.

"Think about it," says Mary Ann. "Joey's mom died, so Joey's dad is all alone. And since my parents are divorced, my mom is all alone." Mary Ann smiles. "If you ask me, they make the perfect pair."

If you ask me, there is nothing perfect about it.

If Mary Ann's mom and Joey's dad go out on a date, they might fall in love.

If they fall in love, they might decide to get married.

If they get married, Mary Ann and Joey

will become step-brother and sister.

If they become step-brother and sister, they will do all kinds of things, like live in the same house together, and eat all their meals together, and go on family vacations together. And they will do all these things . . . WITHOUT ME!

Mary Ann taps me on the head. "Isn't it so, so, so great that my mom and Joey's dad are going out on a date?"

I nod my head yes, that I do think it is great. But I don't think it's great at all. In fact, I think it is terrible, even worse than cutting off my bangs. Mary Ann and her mom came to see me on my birthday. They didn't come so Mary Ann's mom could go out on a date with Joey's dad.

Mary Ann and I get into bed, and she reaches up and turns off the light. "Watch out for bedbugs!" says Mary Ann.

I say it back, because that's what we always say to each other at pajama parties. But as I put my head on my pillow, I don't think about bedbugs. I think about our pajama party, and all I can think is that the best-pajama-party-ever just turned into the worst-pajama-party-ever.

HIGHS AND WOES

"Who wants pizza, and who wants . . . "
Crystal, our Saturday-night babysitter,
looks around the kitchen, then finishes her
sentence. "Pizza?" She laughs at her joke.
She knows all there is to pick from is pizza.

"I'll have the . . . " Joey pretends to
consider his choices. "Pizza," he says in a
funny voice. Then he cracks up.

"Hmmm," says Mary Ann, like she can't decide what she wants. "I think I'll have . . . pizza too." She laughs along with Joey.

Even Winnie and Max smile like they think the whole pizza thing is funny.

"Everyone sure is in a good mood tonight," says Crystal.

Make that *almost* everyone.

I must be the only kid on Wish Pond Road who is not in a good mood. I pull my headband down over my forehead.

"Guess who's going out on a date tonight?" Joey says to Crystal.

Crystal puts a slice of pizza on a paper plate. "Give me a hint."

"He lives in my house. He's bald. And he's not my grandfather," says Joey.

Crystal laughs. "Gee, this is a tough one. I would say your dad, but he never goes out on dates."

"He is tonight," says Mary Ann. "He's going out with my mom!"

Crystal pretends like she's looking into a crystal ball. "I see a fancy restaurant. I see flowers. I see candles. I see true love!"

Crystal thinks she is a fortune-teller. Sometimes, I think she knows what she's

talking about. But not this time. She can't know that Joey's dad and Mary Ann's mom are going to fall in love. She just met Mary Ann and her mom tonight for the first time.

I take a slice of pizza out of the box, go into the living room, and sit down on the couch with Cheeseburger.

Maybe Mary Ann, Joey, Winnie, Max, and even Crystal are happy about Mary Ann's mom and Joey's dad going out on a date, but I'm not.

My mom and Mary Ann's mom spent the whole day talking about it.

What should Mary Ann's mom wear? How should she do her hair? What color should she paint her nails?

Dad was on the phone all afternoon trying to make a reservation at a restaurant.

Did they want French? Or maybe

Italian? Should they go at seven or at eight?

Mary Ann and Joey and Winnie talked all day about their parents going out.

What if they like each other? What if they really, really, really like each other?

All anybody talked about today was "The Date." But if you ask me, they were talking about the wrong date. The date they should have been talking about is my birth date. It seems like everyone around here has forgotten that I'm turning nine in two days.

Especially Mary Ann! She came here to celebrate my birthday, and I think she has forgotten that I'm even having one.

I take a bite of pizza. I hear everyone in the kitchen laughing. I rub Cheeseburger's back. "I guess it's just you and me," I say to my cat.

"Hey," says Crystal. She sits down beside me. "Why the gloomy face?"

I shrug my shoulders and take another bite of pizza.

Crystal looks at me, then she pretends to look into her crystal ball again.

But I don't give her a chance to predict my future. "It's like this," I explain to Crystal. "My birthday is on Monday. This is my birthday weekend and not one single thing is going the way it's supposed to."

Crystal starts to say something, but I don't let her.

"And to make matters worse, everyone is having a good time. Everyone except for one person, and that one person is ME!"

"Mallory," Crystal says. But I stop her. I pull my headband down on my forehead and point to the spot where my bangs used to be.

Crystal looks me in the eye. "Mallory,

your bangs will grow. And I don't need a crystal ball to tell me what's wrong with you. What you have is a bad case of highs and woes."

I'm not sure I want to know, but I ask anyway. "What are highs and woes?"

"Think of it like this," Crystal explains. "Sometimes when you feel good, you feel like you're high up in the air. It seems like your feet are barely touching the ground, and your head is way up in the clouds. And sometimes, when you feel bad, you feel low, like your whole body is crawling around in the dirt."

Sometimes I think Crystal is the weirdest babysitter in Fern Falls. "Well, wouldn't that be called *highs and lows*, not *highs and woes*?" I ask Crystal.

Crystal shakes her head, like she's an old, wise woman who's about to explain something to me. "You have to understand the difference between *lows* and *woes*."

I raise an eyebrow. Crystal is going to tell me the difference between *lows* and *woes*, whether I want to know or not.

"*Lows* are when you feel badly about something. But *woes* are different. *Woes* are when you feel badly about something, and everybody else feels good about it, which makes you feel even worse." Crystal gets a serious look on her face. "Do you understand what I'm saying?"

I rub my forehead. "I guess," I mumble without looking up. Somehow listening to Crystal tell me I have *woes* makes me feel even worse.

Crystal puts her arm around me. "Cheer up, Mal," she says.

"I'll try," I tell Crystal.

But I feel woe . . . as woe as you can go.

BIRTHDAY WISHES

I run my fingers through the pebbles on the edge of the wish pond. I see white and gray pebbles. What I don't see are shiny, little black pebbles, otherwise known as wish pebbles.

When I moved to Wish Pond Road, Joey told me that when you find a wish pebble and throw it into the wish pond, your wish is supposed to come true.

It sounds simple, but wish pebbles are hard to find, especially when you need one. And right now, I need one.

I pick up the closest thing I can find that looks like a wish pebble. I close my eyes and start to make a wish. But when I do, my wish turns into a wish list.

I wish my birth month had gone like I had planned it to.

I wish I hadn't cut off my bangs.

I wish Mary Ann's mom and Joey's dad hadn't gone out on a date.

I wish they won't go out on another one.

I start to throw my stone in the wish pond, then I think about my skating party tomorrow. Even though my wish list is long, I add another one to it.

I wish Mom had planned a surprise party for me. I can't help thinking about how much fun it would be to walk into a party and be super surprised.

I squeeze the stone in the palm of my hand. I'm about to throw it in the wish pond when I hear someone sit down beside me. I open one eye. It's Dad. "How did you know I was here?" I ask him.

Dad sits down beside me. "I heard the front door open. Mom, Max, Mary Ann, her mom, Champ, and Cheeseburger were all asleep in their beds. The only one I couldn't find was you. I thought you might be out here."

I cross my arms.

"What are you doing out here by yourself so early in the morning?"

"Making wishes," I tell Dad.

Dad picks up a stone and throws it into the pond. "Feel like talking about what you're wishing for?"

I look down at the pebble in my hand. "If I tell, my wishes might not come true."

"Sometimes talking about things is better than wishing for them," says Dad.

I close my fingers around the pebble in my hand. "I don't know where to start."

"How about the beginning?" says Dad.

I think about my wish list. My long, long, long wish list. Then I take a deep breath and start. "I worked so hard to plan the perfect birth month celebration," I tell Dad. "And nothing happened like it was supposed to."

"Mallory, I know you expected things to happen a certain way during your birth

month, and they didn't. I know that's disappointing."

"But that's not all." I reach up and feel my forehead. "I was just trying to look like a nine-year-old, and look what happened to my hair."

Dad puts his arm around me. "Sweet Potato, it'll grow back."

Then I tell Dad how scared I am about Mary Ann's mom and Joey's dad liking each other. "I wish they hadn't gone out on a date."

"But they did," says Dad. "And you can't change that."

"Did they have a good time?" I cross my toes and hope Dad says *no.*

But he nods his head *yes.* "They had a very nice time together," says Dad.

This is not what I wanted to hear.

"Do you think they'll go out again?" I ask.

Dad looks down at me. "Yes, I do."

I kick my foot against a pile of rocks on the side of the wish pond. "What if they fall in love and get married, and Mary Ann and Joey become brother and sister, and they're together all the time without me?"

"Sweet Potato, there are some things you can control, and some things you can't. And when you can't control something, you just have to accept it."

Dad tilts my face up so I'm looking at him. "Do you understand what I'm trying to tell you?"

I shake my head no. I'm not sure I do.

"Mallory, things didn't happen the way you expected them to. You might wish that things could have been different, but you can't change what happened."

I think about what Dad said. I can't change what happened during my birth month. I can't make my bangs reappear. I can't do anything about the fact that Mary Ann's mom and Joey's dad went out on a date, and that they might go out on another one.

But there is something I *can* change. "Thanks Dad, you gave me a great idea!"

Dad smiles at me. "Glad I could help."

I stand up and start to go home. Then I stop.

I squeeze the rock in my hand, then throw it into the wish pond. *I wish my birthday party will be the best surprise party in the whole world.*

And I'm planning to make sure that it is.

MALLORY ON HER OWN

"You want to plan your own surprise party?"

"No," I explain to Mary Ann. "I want *you* to plan it." I sit down on the bed next to her. "And I'll be your assistant."

Mary Ann looks confused. "But if you're my assistant, everybody will know that you know about the surprise."

"That's the thing," I whisper to Mary Ann. "No one will know I'm your assistant . . . no one but you."

Mary Ann winks at me. "I get it. You're going to be my *secret* assistant."

"Exactly!" I say. Then I stop to think for a minute. "There's just one more problem. How are you going to tell my mom that you're planning a surprise party when she's already planned a skating party?"

"Simple," says Mary Ann. "I'll tell her that you really want a surprise party and as your lifelong best friend, I want to make one for you."

Mary Ann makes it sound simple, but I'm not sure it will be. "Don't you think my mom will be upset when she finds out I don't want to have the party she planned?"

Mary Ann shrugs. "I'm sure she'll understand when I explain it to her."

I'm not so sure Mom will understand. She didn't understand when I told her I wanted to celebrate my birth month. She didn't understand when I said I wanted to get my ears pierced. I'm not sure she'll understand this either.

Mary Ann leans over and taps me on the head with a pencil. "Earth to Mallory. We've got a lot to do to plan a surprise party before tomorrow."

She closes the door to my room and sits down at my desk. "Let's make a list of everything we need."

I sit down on my bed with Cheeseburger. Mary Ann starts writing.

"Invitations," says Mary Ann. "We need to tell everybody that your party has changed from a skating party to a surprise party."

"We can make our own." I show Mary

Ann a picture in a magazine of party invitations shaped like paper fans.

Mary Ann claps her hands together when she sees it. "They'll be so cute!"

I nod. They will be cute, but there's a problem. "How will we get them to people in time for the party?"

Mary Ann rubs her chin. "Joey can deliver them for us."

"Now, let's talk about food," says Mary Ann.

"I can make peanut butter and marshmallow sandwiches and lemonade," I say.

"You better let me make them," says Mary Ann. "You don't want anyone to see you making your own party food."

Mary Ann is right. I don't want to spoil my own surprise. "But we still need a cake," I remind her. "Do you know how to bake a cake?"

Mary Ann scratches her head. "Your mom will bring the cake. When I tell her about the party, I'll remind her to bring the cake." Mary Ann looks down at the piece of paper in her lap. "What about party favors?"

I reach over and open the drawer to my nightstand.

I take out a bookmark with a big *M* on it. "We can make bookmarks with everyone's initials on them, and then decorate them with glitter and bows."

"Great idea!" says Mary Ann. "There's just one thing left to do."

"What's that?" I ask.

Mary Ann lowers her voice. "We have to figure out how we're going to surprise you."

I think for a minute. Figuring out how to surprise myself is harder than making invitations and party favors.

I snap my fingers. "I've got it. I'll pretend like I'm getting ready for my skating party. When it's time to go, I'll walk into the living room in my skating clothes and you'll have everybody waiting there to surprise me."

"Perfect!" says Mary Ann. She looks at her watch. "We better get busy or we

won't get everything done by tomorrow.
I'll go talk to your mom and Joey. You
start folding fans."

Mary Ann leaves my room. I reach into
my drawer, take out thick sheets of
construction paper, and start folding.

Part of me can't wait to be surprised.
But part of me feels like planning my own
surprise party might not be such a good
idea. I hope Mom isn't upset when Mary
Ann talks to her.

I keep folding fans. When Mary Ann
comes back into my room, my bed is
covered with colorful fans. "Wow!" says
Mary Ann. "These look great."

"Now all we have to do is write the
party information on them, decorate
them, and tie ribbons through the bottoms
of them," I tell her.

"Joey is ready to deliver them," says

Mary Ann. "And your mom is bringing the cake."

I look up. "Did my mom seem upset when you told her about the party?"

Mary Ann ties a ribbon through the bottom of a fan. "She didn't say she was."

I sprinkle glitter across a yellow fan. Just because Mom didn't say she was upset doesn't mean she's not. I really hope she understands that I want to have a surprise party, and I hope she's OK with that.

When we're finished with the invitations, Mary Ann takes them next door to Joey.

When she comes back, Mary Ann and I start on the bookmarks. We work all morning until Mom knocks on my door. "Time for lunch, girls."

"Remember," I whisper to Mary Ann, "not a word about this to my mom. I don't want her to know I'm in on this."

Mary Ann holds up two fingers like she's making a promise. "It's our secret."

After lunch, Mary Ann and I go back to making bookmarks. "Do you think we'll ever finish?" I ask her.

"Maybe you should finish in here," says Mary Ann. "I'll go make the lemonade and sandwiches." Mary Ann winks at me. "I'll tell your mom you're taking a nap."

By the time Mary Ann and I get ready for bed, we are both tired from all the party planning. "Thanks for everything," I tell Mary Ann as we put on our matching yellow peace-sign pajamas. "I thought I would have to plan my party on my own. But I should have known I could count on you."

Mary Ann smiles at me. "I think this will be the best surprise ever." She turns off the light.

I try to go to sleep, but something is bothering me. I turn the light back on.

Mary Ann sits up. "What's the matter?"

"We forgot something," I tell her.

Mary Ann shakes her head. "We have invitations, favors, and food."

"Clothes!" I say to Mary Ann. "I'm the party girl and I need just the right outfit to

look like I'm going skating."

"Hmmm." Mary Ann looks at me. "Why don't you wear something yellow."

"Good idea," I say to Mary Ann. I get my yellow jeans and matching sweater out of my closet. "Yellow is a perfect party color."

Mary Ann nods, like she agrees. "Watch out for bedbugs!" she says.

"You too," I say. But I'm so tired from all our party planning that I don't think my eyes can stay open long enough to look for bedbugs. I turn out the light and put my head down on the pillow.

"Cheeseburger," I whisper, "I can't wait to be surprised."

SURPRISES!

"Mallory, wake up!"

For a minute, I think I'm being attacked by bedbugs. But when I open my eyes, it's just Mom. "What's the matter?" I ask her.

"Do you know what day it is today?" she asks me.

I have to think for a minute. "Monday?"

"It's Monday," says Mom. "But do you know why this Monday is different than all other Mondays?"

I roll over and look at the clock on my nightstand. It's so early!

"Mom, on all other Mondays, we have school, but today we don't. What's so important about this Monday that you needed to wake me up so early?"

"I think you'll be very excited when you hear what I have to say." Mom sits down on the bed beside me. "Today is your birthday, and I have a surprise for you!"

I think about the surprise party I'm having this afternoon. "A surprise?" I ask Mom.

"Why don't I show you," she says. Mom ties a bandanna around my eyes, then helps me out of bed. I can feel her leading me down the hall.

"Where are we going?" I ask. I can't imagine where she would be taking me so early in the morning in my pajamas.

Mom stops walking. "Would you like to see your surprise?"

I nod. Mom unties the bandanna. When she takes it off, I am surprised . . . VERY SURPRISED!

"HAPPY BIRTHDAY, MALLORY!" shout my friends and my family.

Mom puts a party hat on my head. I look around the living room and can't believe what I'm seeing! Dad, Max, Mary Ann, her mom, Joey, Winnie, Mr. Winston, Crystal, Pamela, and all my friends from school are there . . . and they're all in their pajamas and robes and slippers! Even Champ and Cheeseburger have on little matching nightcaps.

"What's going on?" I ask.

Mom grins. "It's a surprise pajama party for you! We all know how much you love pajama parties."

"And surprise parties!" says Mary Ann.

"But what about my skating party?"

Mom gives me a big hug. "There never was a skating party."

I can't believe it! "There never was a skating party?"

Mom shakes her head. "Dad and I wanted to make sure you would be really surprised." I am really surprised *and* really confused.

"What about the party Mary Ann and I planned? What happened to the invitations we made?" I look at Joey. "The ones you delivered yesterday?"

Joey smiles. "I delivered the

invitations . . . to your mom."

"And I hid them in the kitchen," Mom says.

I can't believe it. "You knew about this?" I say to Joey.

He grins. "I can be a very good secret keeper."

And there's another good secret keeper too. I look at Mary Ann. "You knew about this and spent the whole day yesterday helping me make invitations and bookmarks and sandwiches. You didn't say a word."

"Joey and I didn't want to spoil the real surprise. We were your mom's assistants." She winks at me. "Her secret assistants."

I throw my arms around Mary Ann and Joey. "You're the best friends a girl could have."

And then I look at all my friends. "You all knew about this and nobody said a word?"

Max smiles. "I guess we're all good secret keepers."

Mary Ann giggles. "Look around."

A sign on the wall says, *Happy Birthday, Mallory!* Streamers and balloons hang from the ceiling. There's a big pile of presents in the corner.

The dining room table is covered with all my favorite breakfast foods: doughnuts and hot chocolate with mini-marshmallows, even the platter of peanut butter and

marshmallow sandwiches that Mary Ann
made.

I pick one up and take a bite. "Mmmmm."

"Don't eat too many sandwiches," says
Mom. "You need to save room for cake."
Dad carries in a tray with the biggest ice
cream cake on it that I've ever seen.

"It's the cake-of-the-year," says Dad.

He puts the cake down on the table and lights the candles. Everybody sings *Happy Birthday*.

"Make a wish," says Mom.

I look at Dad, and we smile at each other. Yesterday at the wish pond, I wished for the best surprise party in the whole world. I close my eyes and blow out my

candles. I feel like my wish is coming true.

Mom cuts the cake and Mary Ann's mom passes around plates.

I take a bite. "Mmmm! Cookies and cream for breakfast is my new favorite."

Dad laughs. "Ice cream for breakfast on birthdays only!"

"Time for games," says Mom when everybody finishes their cake.

We play *Pin the Slippers on the Sheep*. It's like *Pin the Tail on the Donkey,* but you have to pin the slippers onto the sheep's feet.

Mom blindfolds Mary Ann and spins her around in a circle. Mary Ann walks toward the wall and pins the slippers on the sheep's nose.

When it's Joey's turn, he doesn't do much better. He pins the slippers on the sheep's ear, and Pamela pins them on his stomach.

Finally, Max pins the slippers in the right

place . . . on the sheep's feet. Mom gives him a pair of fuzzy yellow slippers as a prize.

Max looks at the slippers like touching them could give him a bad disease. "The birthday girl can have these." He hands me the slippers.

I slip them on my feet. "They look perfect with my pj's!"

I give Max a hug. "You're the best brother a girl could have."

Max rolls his eyes. "On your birthday, only!"

When we finish playing *Pin the Slippers on the Sheep,* Mom holds up a glass jar of jelly beans. "Who wants to play *Guess the Number of Jelly Beans in the Jar?*"

I look at the jar of jelly beans in Mom's

hands. Then I look at the pile of presents. It's hard to focus on jelly beans when they're near a pile of presents.

Pamela looks at me. "I think the only game Mallory wants to play is called *Open the Presents!*"

I laugh. Pamela knows me really well. Then I give her a hug. "You're the best desk mate in all of Fern Falls!"

Mom piles all the boxes on the living room floor, and everybody sits in a circle around me.

"Open this one first," says Danielle. "It's from Arielle and me."

I open a big pink box filled with makeup. "It's a makeover kit," says Danielle. "It's what you need if you want a new look."

I thank Danielle and Arielle, but I give Mary Ann a secret smile. I've had enough new looks to last me for a while.

I keep opening presents. Mary Ann gives
me a ninth birthday scrapbook. It has nine
hearts on the cover. "One for each year,"
says Mary Ann.

"I love it!" I tell her.

Joey and Winnie give me a new pair of
roller blades. "Now you have your own
skates," says Joey. "And they're purple,"
says Winnie.

"Wow! I can't believe you got me

these!" I take off my fuzzy yellow slippers and try on my new roller blades.

"Now we can go skating," says Joey.

I grin. "Sounds like fun."

I keep opening presents.

Pamela gives me a glow-in-the-dark paper weight. Crystal gives me a days-of-the-week set of headbands.

Mom and Dad give me new pajamas with birthday cakes all over them. "You can celebrate your birthday every time you wear these," says Dad.

Then Max hands me a box. It's big, but it's not heavy. When I shake it, it doesn't make a sound. "I can't imagine what's in here," I say to my brother.

"It's not really for you," says Max. "But I think you'll like it."

Now, I'm really curious. I rip off the wrapping paper and open the box. Inside,

there's a new cat bed for Cheeseburger . . .
and it matches my bed!

"I love it!" I say to Max. I try to hug him.
He ducks, so I miss. But he smiles at me.

"I hope you have a great year!" says Max.

Mom passes out the party favors she
bought. "Mini flashlights," she says, "so
you can read in your pajamas in bed."

Then Mary Ann gives everyone the
bookmarks we made.

After all of the guests have gone, Mom
picks up the tray with the leftover birthday
cake on it. "Did you like your party?" she
asks me.

I scratch my head, like I have to think
hard to answer the question she just asked
me. "Well, it wasn't exactly what I
expected."

Dad looks concerned. "Sometimes," he
says, "you don't get what you expected."

I stop scratching and start smiling. "And sometimes, what you get is even better than what you expected."

Mom puts the cake down. She and Dad both smile.

I hug them both. "Mom, Dad, thanks so much for everything. I loved my party."

"Surprises are fun," says Dad.

I smile at my parents. "Especially when you're really surprised."

"Speaking of surprises," says Dad. "There's another one, and I think I hear it outside."

I run to the front window. Grandma's car is pulling into our driveway. "Grandma!" I scream.

Everyone follows me outside.

When Grandma gets out of her car, I fling myself around her. "I can't believe it! *You're* what you sent for my birthday!"

Grandma hugs me so hard she crushes my party hat. "I didn't wear pajamas, but I did bring your present . . . in person!" She hands me a box wrapped in purple tissue paper.

I shake the box, but it doesn't make a sound. I rip off the paper and open the lid. Inside, there's a pillow that has the number nine inside a big heart.

I hug my pillow. "It's perfect," I tell Grandma. "I've only been nine for a few minutes, but I love it already! It's definitely full of surprises." I take a deep breath and try to straighten my mashed party hat. "I never thought I'd say this, but I think I've had enough surprises for one day."

Everyone laughs. Then Mary Ann's mom comes over to me. "Actually," she says, "I have one more." She hands me a small box.

I think about my new scrapbook. "But Mary Ann already gave me a present."

"This one's from me," says Mary Ann's mom. "And I think you'll really like it."

I clutch the small box in my hands. When I shake it, something rattles. I don't know what's inside, but I can't wait to find out.

THE REST OF
THE HOLE STORY

When I get to school, I hand Mrs. Daily
a sheet of paper. "You didn't ask me to
write this, but I thought you might like
reading it."

"I'm always proud of my students when
they do extra work," says Mrs. Daily. Then
she smiles at me. "And I can't wait to read
the rest of the story!"

The Rest of the Hole Story
by Mallory McDonald
N.T.R. (No Tissues Required)

I know you must remember our story,
which ended when the heroine was
wiping away her tears because her
mother refused to grant her one,
actually two, small requests she made on
her ninth birthday.

I'm sure you can't forget that whole
you-have-to-wait-until-you're-twelve-
to-get-your-ears-pierced speech.

Well, after the girl was forced to listen
to that speech, she went to her room.
Actually, she was sent there.

She made a wish for a miracle to
happen, and to her surprise and
amazement, it did! Her fairy godmother
(actually her lifelong best friend's

mother) gave her a pair of earrings for her birthday.

Of course, the little girl gave them right back and said she didn't need them because her mother wouldn't let her get her ears pierced.

But the girl's fairy godmother just smiled and told her that she explained to the girl's mother that waiting until you're twelve to get your ears pierced, especially when you've just cut off your bangs, didn't seem necessary.

And the girl's mother agreed!!! (I hope you didn't faint when you read this!)

So the fairy godmother drove the girl and the girl's best friend to the mall. (Unfortunately, they had to go in a minivan, not in a golden coach, but what happened next was so exciting, the girl didn't care.)

When she got to the mall, she got her ears pierced!

And everybody lived happily ever after. Especially the girl.

The End

P.S. In most fairy tales, the heroine falls in love with a handsome prince, but in this one, the fairy godmother falls for the man next door. At first, the heroine was pretty upset about this. She was worried about what it meant for her future. But her fairy godmother told the heroine to stop worrying about the future and start picking out earrings. And that's exactly what the heroine did. She picked out heart-shaped earrings and so did her best friend. They vowed to always wear matching earrings.

MALLORY'S PARTY PLANNING KIT

Birthdays are a big deal! Here are some things you can do to make your birthday party extra special!

INVITATIONS

You can make your own invitations shaped like fans. Just follow these four simple steps:

Step 1: Fold a piece of paper into the shape of a fan.

Step 2: On the folds of the paper, write the time, date, and place of your party.

Step 3: Decorate your invitations with paint, markers, and stickers.

Step 4: Deliver your invitations to your friends!

PARTY FAVORS

Handmade bookmarks are super cool. Just cut out paper in the shape of a bookmark. Then draw each guest's initial on the bookmark. Decorate the bookmarks with ribbons and glitter. Every time your friends open their books, they will remember your great party.

THANK-YOU NOTES

Don't forget the thank-you notes! I
think the *fill-in-the-blank* ones are the best.
You can decorate them so they match your
invitations. Here's what mine looked like:

Dear (<u>person's name you're thanking</u>
<u>goes here</u>),

Thank you so, so, so much for the super
(<u>fill in the gift you received</u>) that you gave
me! I really, really, really love it! I am so,
so, so glad you could come to my party.

Thanks again! Extra big huge hugs
and kisses!

(<u>Just sign your name</u>)

P.S. (I always put a P.S.! It gives you a
chance to say something nice about the gift!)

And if you're thinking that writing thank-you notes isn't as much fun as other activities (like getting presents), you and I think a lot alike! But you have to do it. And you have to do it pretty soon after your party, or your mother (if she's anything like mine) will start saying: *"(Fill in your name here!), have you written those notes yet?"*

Trust me, you don't want your mom to start saying that!

Well, I hope you like some of these ideas, and I hope when your birthday rolls around it is super special! I know mine was.

I'm already thinking about my next birthday. I know it's a year away, but I'm turning ten, which is a VERY big deal!

I just love birthdays! Don't you?

Carolrhoda Books, Inc.
A division of Lerner Publishing Group
241 First Avenue North
Minneapolis, MN 55401 U.S.A.

Website address: www.lernerbooks.com

Library of Congress Cataloging-in-Publication Data

Friedman, Laurie B.,
    Happy birthday, Mallory! / by Laurie Friedman ; illustrations by Tamara Schmitz.
        p.   cm.
    Summary: After a difficult year, Mallory plans a month-long celebration of her ninth birthday in hopes that her next year will be wonderful.
        ISBN-13: 978-1-57505-823-8 (lib. bdg. : alk. paper)
        ISBN-10: 1-57505-823-5 (lib. bdg. : alk. paper)
        [1. Birthdays—Fiction.] I. Schmitz, Tamara, ill. II. Title.
    PZ7.F89773Hap 2005
    [Fic]—dc22   2004031080

Manufactured in the United States of America
1 2 3 4 5 6 — BP — 10 09 08 07 06 05